Camp Nine

Camp Nine

A Novel

Vivienne Schiffer

The University of Arkansas Press
Fayetteville
2011

Manufactured in the United States of America

ISBN-10: 1-55728-645-0
ISBN-13: 978-1-55728-645-1

17 16 15 14 13 5 4 3 2 1

Designed by Liz Lester

⊗ The paper used in this publication meets the minimum requirements of the American National Standard for Permanence of Paper for Printed Library Materials Z39.48-1984.

LIBRARY OF CONGRESS CATALOGING-IN-PUBLICATION DATA

Schiffer, Vivienne, 1959–
Camp nine / Vivienne Schiffer.
p. cm.
ISBN 978-1-55728-972-8 (cloth : alk. paper)
1. Japanese Americans—Evacuation and relocation, 1942–1945—Fiction.
2. Arkansas—Fiction. I. Title.
PS3619.C366C36 2011
813'.6—dc23

2011029104

ACKNOWLEDGMENTS

Although it was inspired by the realities of the Japanese American internment camp experience in Arkansas, *Camp Nine* is purely fictional. It is true that I was born and largely raised in Rohwer, Arkansas, and the fictional town of Rook that *Camp Nine* describes is very much like the Rohwer of my childhood. We did live next to my grandparents, who were prosperous planters. But they were kind and generous people, as was my late father's only sister, who was and is the complete opposite of the aunt in *Camp Nine*. No parallels between these characters and real people should be drawn. The same must be said for all the characters of *Camp Nine*.

Many people were responsible for *Camp Nine* seeing the light of day. First was Valerie West, my extraordinary screenwriting professor at the University of California at Los Angeles, who insisted I must tell a story based on the improbability of nearly ten thousand Americans of Japanese descent suddenly appearing in the Arkansas Delta during the 1940s. But it would never have gone any farther than my imagination had it not been for the support of my wonderful agent, Brettne Bloom of Kneerim and Williams, who continued to believe in this story when many others would have given up. Many thanks, also, to Lorna Owen, whose kind words and encouragement kept me going, and whose editorial prowess whipped earlier drafts into prime shape.

I will always be grateful to Larry Malley of the University of Arkansas Press, who, despite his unfortunate Yankee upbringing, got down here to the South as fast as he could and continues to make it a better place. And especially to David Stricklin of the Butler

Center for Arkansas Studies for his interest in Arkansas's internment camps and his kindness to my family.

Mary and Laine Lindsey read the first draft of *Camp Nine* and not only provided marvelous feedback, but offered unbridled enthusiasm. I'm indebted to my friends at Thompson and Knight, among them Bill McDonald, David Furlow, Jim Cousar, Nichole Olajuwon, and Marlen Whitley. And Brettne wouldn't have been possible without her lovely parents, Steve and Janis Block.

So many people were there during the writing of *Camp Nine* offering encouragement, including Rick and Cindy Trevathan, Terrye Dees, Bill and Beth Maher, Diane Hernandez, Ken and Anita Magidson, Gus and Callie Saper, Diane Anderson, James Lowe, and Donna Hammond. Thank you all.

I also want to express my gratitude to my new friend, John Carrithers, for his appreciation of the beauty of the Rohwer camp site and the significance of what happened there so many decades ago.

Unlimited thanks to my mother, Rosalie Santine Gould, who inspired so much of *Camp Nine*, and without whose efforts to preserve the Japanese American experience in Arkansas, the memories would have stayed fragmented and been forever lost. Thanks also to my brothers, Clayton Gould and Mitch Gould, for sharing our Rohwer childhood.

But no words can completely express my gratitude to and for my family: my sons Adam, Jake, and Wyatt; my daughter, Samantha; my daughter-in-law, Libby; my son-in-law, Shawn; my grandsons, Kai and Braiden; my niece, Liz; and my nephew, Gifford.

As much as I love and appreciate everyone on this page, however, if I could only mention one person to whom I owe everything, here he is: my husband, Paul Schiffer. Thank you, Paul, for supporting everything I set my mind to doing. I love you.

This book is dedicated with love and devotion to the Infant of Prague.

Camp Nine

APPLICATION FOR LEAVE CLEARANCE:

QUESTION #27:

Are you willing to serve in the armed forces of the United States on combat duty, wherever ordered?

QUESTION #28:

Will you swear unqualified allegiance to the United States of America and faithfully defend the United States from any or all attack by foreign or domestic forces, and forswear any form of allegiance or obedience to the Japanese Emperor or any other foreign government, power, or organization?

Rook, Arkansas, 1965

These are the parts of my life: before Camp Nine and after Camp Nine, and those brief, unexpected days when Camp Nine was everything to me. That I was only a child then, and that most of the details that make a person whole still lay before me, doesn't change things. When I look back, everything is divided into those three, distinct times.

I sit on a concrete bench in the shade of a cherry tree, now a graceful giant, its black branches adorned with the pale pink blossoms that will last only a few days, my eyes trained down the single lane dirt road that leads to the railroad tracks. A decaying brick smokestack rises at the edge of the bayou, one of the last reminders that there was once a city on this empty plot of land.

Camp Nine is gone. As a girl teetering on adulthood, I watched it disintegrate, vanishing just as quickly as it had come, until all that remained were the field and my memories. I own this land now. And I own those memories, which I guard carefully, even from those closest to me.

I check my watch again. David's telegram said nothing more than that he would arrive today sometime after noon, and it is now one thirty. His cryptic message, delivered in short bursts of words like Morse code, simply said when, not why. With nowhere to reply, I am left to wonder.

Like everyone who watches television and reads *Life* magazine, I know that David Matsui lives a fashionable life in London, where his concerts entertain royalty and his shows sell out the Royal Albert Hall. The official story of his rise to fame recounts his improbable discovery one night at a Chicago club while he worked in a meat-packing plant by day, his virtuosity at the guitar, and his meteoric popularity among that new breed of snobs known as blues purists. But Camp Nine is never a part of the story. Famously private, David doesn't talk about his parents, or his older brother, who was once his hero and his best friend.

But I'm guilty of harboring his secret as well. Although I live a scant ten miles from where rows upon rows of barracks once stood, my husband and daughters have only the vaguest idea of what happened at Camp Nine, and perhaps sensing my reluctance to open up about certain events in my past, they never plumb me for details. I have never mentioned David Matsui's name.

None of us who were there ever speaks of what happened during those strange, anxious months, as if the whole affair were a dream that didn't come true. But the Delta is mysterious, the kind of place where so many things happen that go unnoticed by the outside world. The overwhelming stillness of the countryside and the oppressive flatness of the terrain, cleared almost entirely now of trees, slow the passage of time. The air is molasses in summer, an iron blanket of cold in the winter. The vast landscape tricks the mind into thinking that gravity is somehow stronger here, that the bayous and the canebrakes can pin you against them so that even light can't escape.

I did my best to break free, choosing a faraway girls' college up north where my slow, languid way of speaking and my narrow, provincial views made me an easy target for the sophisticated girls from Boston and Philadelphia. Their scoffs and sneers were a shock to me, since my mother and I had passed for liberal thinkers down in the Delta. I stayed away only as long as I had to, then gazed out the window with anticipation the whole of the long, last train ride home, my pulse slowing once the familiar scenery came into view.

I can't imagine what David wants after all this time. He spent the entirety of his days at Camp Nine struggling to get away, and as the years passed with no word from him, I often wondered if he ever thought of us. His telegram gave me the answer to that much, at least. There were times when I longed to find him. I wanted to ask him how he could have turned his back on everything that had happened. But it was pride that kept me from reaching out. After all we had done for David and his family, everything I thought we had meant to them, if they didn't think enough of us to have kept in touch, well, then what was the point?

But my nerves have gotten the better of me now. Whatever his reasons for coming, I have my own for anxiously awaiting him. And as a plume of dust appears on the horizon and a car snakes its way toward me, I remember when it all began.

Chapter 1

To understand the story, one must understand the place, for the events could not have transpired anywhere else. Just as the beginning of life itself was dependent on the peculiar environment that made possible its first spark and flash, the story of Camp Nine is a product of the surroundings in which it occurred.

The afternoon it happened, in July of 1942, my mother and I had taken our dinner of watermelon and toast on the porch. Both the menu and the location were, in themselves, manifestations of that custom known as summer, where conversations were shorter and slower. The heat, a tiresome, unwelcome guest in every room, drove us outdoors into the shade whenever possible, and dictated a conservation of energy from the earliest hours. It spread over us at sunrise, informing our dreams before we'd even roused from sleep, and sapped our strength at noontime. By suppertime, few philosophies were so keenly felt that one could be compelled to expend the breath to argue. Even our nighttimes, spent tossing in our beds, were made fitful by the heaviness of the air.

I was an odd child, tall for my age and gangly, the color of October wheat. My plain features were not improved by my uneven, homemade pageboy haircut. I might have found comfort in having inherited the exotic black silk of my mother's hair or the patrician blond of my father, but I was dealt instead a mousy and unremarkable brown. My eyes were the deepest, impenetrable black, the kind that took in light but reflected nothing in return. Everything about me seemed to fade into the wallpaper around me. I studied my beautiful mother's habits, observing her closely for clues on how I, too, could be as fine a lady as she, but it seemed then impossible to attain. I could follow her, but only as a shadow.

She was a lovely woman, despite the gray, shirtwaist dress she wore as regularly as a uniform. In those days before Camp Nine changed everything, gray and black were the only colors I recall her wearing, as if she were still in mourning for my father, who by then had been dead for more than five years, or trying to mask the fact that she had once been, and still was, regarded as a great beauty. Her dark eyes were the shape of almonds, and her thick brows were curved and peaked, giving her the appearance when she spoke of being extraordinarily attentive. She wore her lush hair pulled back loosely, the ends curling slightly across the plain fabric on her shoulders.

Mother and I took our dinner in small, languid bites. My thoughts at that moment are frozen in time: I was studying a red wasp navigating the spiny crown of a purple coneflower. I don't know what Mother was thinking. She was probably already contemplating what we would have for our supper. In any event, the last normal, ordinary thing that happened was that my grandfather's black Lincoln Continental emerged from the cypress bend in Rook Lane and barreled past in a cloud of dust. The wall clock inside our living room sounded once to note the hour.

Mother shook her head. "Dinner time in the big house. You can set your watch by Walter's stomach."

No matter where in the county he was when dinner time approached, my grandfather appeared every day precisely at one o'clock, as if he had internal springs and dials. The Lincoln slowed and bounced up into the concrete drive across our gate, disappearing from view behind a grove of oaks.

Mother and Grandpa feuded famously, about things trivial and important alike. Though she was only his daughter-in-law, I now realize they were more alike than not, but at the time that was one of the many things about which I was unaware. I was just twelve that summer, but Mother often treated me as if I were much older, probably because she had no one else with whom to share her thoughts. She had confided in me that her latest quarrel with Grandpa was over Hammond Ryfle, our plantation foreman.

Mr. Ryfle was supposed to have already cleared Mother's hundred acres upstream of Black Bayou, but spring had come and had passed without him attending to it. He was, instead, occupied with clearing the poorest of my late father's land, a large plot of virgin timber and swamp that was known as Camp Nine. He swore it was on instruction by Grandpa, whose refusal to answer Mother's questions aggravated her like a knotted neck muscle. Just seeing Grandpa's Lincoln pass caused her lips to draw up tight.

"Is Mr. Ryfle all done at Camp Nine?" I asked.

Mother leaned back and set her plate, littered with rind and crust, on one of the glass-topped wicker end tables that flanked the flowery cushioned swing. "I saw him driving the bulldozer off yesterday," she said, flicking a stray crumb from her lap into her hand and crushing it with a napkin. "It's too late to plant anything, but I suppose he could start laying by the fields. I don't know what Walter's got planned." She gathered a corner of the napkin and worried it into the table, wiping the ring left by her iced tea glass. "I quit asking."

We rocked for a few minutes, occupied by our own thoughts in the pleasant quiet, but then it happened. A faint sound rose in the distance, down Highway 1, a tiny rippling of the air that was unfamiliar. We looked at each other, Mother frowning.

"What's that?" I asked.

She blinked in consternation, less alarmed than puzzled. "Sirens?" she ventured.

Try as I might now, I can't say that I had ever heard a siren anywhere other than from the radio shows I loved to listen to at night, while the crickets sang outside. There was no police force or hospital in our town of Rook. We never had emergencies that required any hurry, and if we had, our lack of basic infrastructure would have left us unable to respond with sirens. But as the alien sound approached, the whirring turned into an ear-splitting cry. I scrambled to the edge of the porch and pressed my nose against the screen, staring through the pale pink and blue hydrangeas, fascinated by the novelty but unwilling to leave the safety of the house.

Two state trooper vehicles passed on the highway, lights flashing. They moved slowly, crawling to a stop at the dirt road that crossed the tracks, leading to Camp Nine. Behind them bundled a line of twenty or thirty trucks, each bearing a long trailer piled with mountains of lumber.

"What on earth?" Mother shouted, wrenching the screen door nearly from its hinges and taking the steps down into the brittle yard. I thought she might be heading on foot to Camp Nine, but as I sprinted behind her, she turned and marched the length of Grandpa's driveway, pausing only once to take in the spectacle of the procession passing through town and vanishing from our sight.

She burst through the door of Grandma's cookhouse and stalked to the middle of the room, but I remained just inside the door, obscuring myself in the shadow of a punched-tin pie safe. Grandpa sat hunched over a wooden table draped by a worn checkered oilcloth. Odessa, my grandmother's housekeeper, stood before the sink, her hands submerged in soapy water. She was startled by our sudden intrusion, but Grandpa pretended to notice nothing.

We were all accustomed to knock-down, drag-out fights between Mother and Grandpa. With his only son dead and gone, Grandpa now had to deal with Mother in matters of my father's estate, which included me. Their sensibilities could not have been more opposed, but I believe that deep down, he admired her spunk and spark. What was certain was that he enjoyed a skirmish with her as much as a good bird hunt.

"Walter?" Mother demanded. "What in hell is going on over there?"

Odessa pulled her hands from the water and ran them over her apron, then made a hasty exit out the back door and onto the wash porch. Grandpa's eyes darted sideways at Mother, but the fork continued its arc into his mouth. He chewed and glanced at a clock. "Less than five minutes," he said, swallowing. "That's some kind of record, even for you, Carrie Morton."

Whatever was happening at Camp Nine was something Grandpa had orchestrated, and she demanded to know what he had planned. In my lifetime, not so much as a new house had been constructed in Rook, and the lumber being delivered that very moment was enough to build an entire city.

Grandpa set down his fork and lifted a linen napkin. "You know, yourself Carrie, that land my son bought has no value for farming. It's as worthless as a Confederate dollar."

"It's not yours," she said.

He waved the napkin at her. "Now don't start that again."

"It belongs to Chess," she said.

"Used to," he said.

In the plantation world in which we lived, land was power. Those with it controlled those without it, pure and simple. I'd overheard snippets of conversations between my mother and our own beloved housekeeper, Ruby Jean Monroe, that I had some measure of fortune of my own, but I'd never known her to address it directly. And now, before I'd even known I was in possession of such entitlement, it was gone, sold out from under me. I backed against the screen and pressed into the door jamb, hoping for more information.

Grandpa lifted his sweating glass of iced tea and took a sip. "Where the hell'd Odessa go? This tea needs sugar." His eyes searched the table for the sugar bowl.

His unwillingness to argue with Mother was a sure sign that she was defeated. She sank into a chair. "You've sold it."

Spying the bowl behind the napkin holder, Grandpa popped two cubes of sugar in his glass and stirred it. "To the gov'ment," he said.

The deal was done, and there was no use in her fussing about it. Although she pressed him, Grandpa refused to answer her questions.

It might have been a military base, but there was already a new airfield near Little Rock, and one of the South's largest military installations, Camp Shelby, was not that far away in Mississippi.

The issue of Grandpa's stewardship of my land aside, we might have welcomed a military presence, we'd grown so fatigued of our own insecurity. In those early days of the war, how were we to know that we wouldn't be invaded, as had Poland and France? Talk had already been growing about the combatants in our midst. There was a new prisoner-of-war camp for Italians fewer than thirty miles to our south. And when Mother asked if Camp Nine were to become a German prisoner-of-war camp, the suggestion seemed to hit pay dirt with Grandpa. The faintest hint of surprise passed underneath his glasses.

"Now, Carrie," he said, settling back in his chair, "it's not my business now. I got a pretty penny for it."

Her face contorted. "Is that all you care about?"

"What else is there to care about? I can't make any money farming it. I told Little Walt not to buy it in the first place. If you'd had any sense, you'd have told him that, too."

"You've lost your mind, Walter Morton."

Their little squabbles had always seemed to be of little consequence. She was a Progressive—my grandmother dismissively called her that to her face, much to Mother's concealed delight. By contrast, it was entirely in Grandpa's best interests that the status quo of our community remain as unchanged as possible. But those were just ideas. This time, ideas translated into things, things we could define. And this time, she could not win. The contest was over before she even knew it had begun. I watched her realization of that fact color her features as we trudged toward home.

It was the first time I understood the ways in which my grandfather controlled us. Other than the small parcels that Mother owned herself, he owned this county, and the crops from that land provided the only income my mother and I had left to live on. Looking back, I should have taken comfort in Grandpa's refusal to be dominated by something as paltry as a world war. To him, that conflict was just another chance to profit. Regardless of the life-and-death struggles being waged on foreign soil, ours was his world, and by that July evening word had spread as far as nearby McHenry that German prisoners of war were coming to Camp Nine.

It had been ten years since our president had told us that we had nothing to fear but fear itself. He'd been speaking of the Great Depression, an event that hardly anyone in DeSoto County had even noticed. Here, where the few of us who were wealthy were exceedingly so and everyone else was desperately poor and always had been, the financial crisis was just a newspaper headline. But the terror and uncertainty that accompanied the war was different. Even though it was being played out across vast oceans, every boy going off to war, every bit of news that filtered back to us of Axis victories, every mention of Pearl Harbor, brought a heightened anxiety about the outcome.

But life had to go on, if not as usual, then as a narrative in which there were repeated threads. Ever since my father's death, my mother had been engaged in silent wars of her own, not just with Grandpa, but also against Hammond Ryfle. As a farmer myself, married to a farmer, I now understand her dilemma. No foreman was going to take orders from a woman. It simply wasn't done, and I'm sad to say not much has changed, at least in that regard. She may have been free to employ someone else, but using my grandfather's foreman gave her some small measure of protection, and she tolerated him as best she could.

On the surface, it seemed Mr. Ryfle tested her patience with his broken promises, baleful conduct, and deceitful talk, and I know she suspected him of keeping more of her crop than he accounted for. But running beneath these complaints was a current of something deeper. They avoided each other, and when they were forced to interact, their exchanges played like a game that had secret rules.

Any visit by Mr. Ryfle or mention of the Ryfle name brought a cloud across my mother's brow, followed by a loud click of her tongue against the back of her teeth, a gesture of derision that she had inherited from her mother. Sometimes, the tension drove her to take to her bed, felled by what she called a sick headache which might last for days. I endured those episodes silently, stoically, choosing not to risk her ire by asking her why she put up with him when she could just hire some other foreman from the levee to work our land.

Instead, I retreated to Ruby Jean. All the questions of life that I needed answered I lay at her tired feet while she ironed. Cornering her while she was involved in a steady, repetitive task made my questions easier to ask, and if she didn't feel like answering or couldn't find a way, easier for her to ignore.

I'd asked about Mr. Ryfle just days before. Ruby Jean sighed and gave the same response, as if my questions were part of a short-answer quiz which she'd already memorized. "Bad blood is what it is," she said, sprinkling the stretched and starched cotton with dots of water from a Coca-Cola bottle, the top of which had been punctured in several places by an ice pick. "It's bad blood that started a long time ago and you best stay out the way of that whole Ryfle family." She propped the hot iron on the edge of the board, twisted her arms about her waist, and began to hum, withdrawing as if just talking about the whole Ryfle affair was bad luck that needed to be opposed by her peculiar combination of Christianity and the voodoo that was still prevalent in the black community that lived along the bayou. Once Ruby Jean was in that place in her mind, there was no use to try further conversation.

Although the Arkansas side of the Delta was more lush and fertile than the Mississippi side, it was still largely wild and possessed none of the graceful history of the Old South. Civilization may have spread west to the Pacific more than a century before, but it had leapfrogged over our little pocket of forest and swamp, leaving us to survive in a different kind of frontier.

In the Arkansas Delta, one's daily encounter with a dozen different things could result in tragic death—from the most common and ordinary things like a rusty nail, a sleepy water moccasin, or a plain fever to the extraordinary, such as a tornado or a laborer, drunk and aggressive after a payday binge. An ordered community, as small as it might have been, was paramount to keeping catastrophe at bay.

At ten thousand acres, the Morton Plantation was the largest in the county and was the hub of that community. My father's mother's family, the Hestons, had acquired large tracts by original grant before the Civil War, but it was my grandfather, Walter Morton Sr., who married into what the Hestons owned, and then bought, traded, or, some have said, flat-out stole the rest and consolidated it into the Morton Plantation. My father, Walter Morton Jr., or Little Walt, as he was known his entire life, was raised in a rarefied world of gentility which my grandparents had pretty much conjured up from thin air.

My mother came, if not from the wrong side of the tracks, then from the wrong side of the bayou. It was not just that Mother's family was poor. Her father, Giorgio Marchi, and her mother, Isabella, began life in Italy, and immigrated to America as part of a trade deal between Italy and certain Southern entrepreneurs. The entrepreneurs could replace the black farm workers they were losing to the industrialized North, and Italy could cull its population of starving peasants. Sold to the Italian farmers as an opportunity to own land and have a better life in America, the Marchi family quickly found that they were no more than indentured servants in a rigged system that was always a step ahead of them. Once Giorgio and Isabella were liberated of their servitude, they struck out of their familial community, buying a small plot of foreclosed farmland in DeSoto County, just outside the boundaries of the Morton Plantation.

Free at last in the new world, Giorgio and Isabella dropped the immigrant marker—the "i" from their name—and raised my mother, their only child, to speak only English. Italian was strictly forbidden. Isabella died of rheumatic fever when my mother was just a small child. Giorgio, overwhelmed with the responsibilities of farming his fifty acres alone with only a mule and wagon, turned to his nearest female neighbor to care for his young daughter in the evenings, after the woman finished her long day working for the almighty Mortons: Ruby Jean Monroe.

It was years before I understood the gulf between my paternal grandparents and my mother. In the complicated system of plantation society, Mother was in no-man's land, neither white nor black, but foreign, technically white but raised by Ruby Jean. That every living need of the Mortons' own child, Little Walt, was met by black women, and that he was taught to ride and hunt and plant cotton by black men, was, in their eyes, a different story. Little Walt was a Morton. My mother, Carolina March Morton, despite her regal bearing and college education, would never be one.

In contrast to Grandma and Grandpa's imposing stone home, it was my mother's choice that we live in the small, white frame house across their gate, despite offers from Grandma and Grandpa for Daddy and her to live with them in the mansion. But I envied the fine, romantic building that seemed to have sprung straight from the imagination of a Brontë sister and I sometimes questioned Mother's choice. "It's cold," she always replied, as if that explained everything. I didn't ever believe that was the real reason, but I had to agree with her assessment. Set far back off the road behind spreading trees, the leaded-glass windows were dark, the stone porch was covered in thick vines, and the walls were so shaded in the summer that lush carpets of violets grew alongside the house and drive.

Our little wooden cottage, with its twin porches and graceful flowering bushes, had a curved doorway that Mother said was inspired by the Norman farmhouses encountered by the soldiers in the Great War in France. It was canopied by four red oaks and a black walnut, but it was sunny and warm, and I was delighted by its storybook appeal.

With a population of not quite ninety, our town of Rook was indeed tiny. It wasn't even a proper town at all, but rather merely a settlement, a small cluster of dwellings nestled beside the rail line. The cotton gin, the grain dryer, and a handful of modest houses were on one side of the railroad tracks, and Mr. Gilwell's general store and the water tower occupied our side. Down a dirt road that wound along the bayou was a clapboard church and cemetery for the black community, all of whom were in the employ of the Mortons.

These and our homes comprised the whole affair, and despite its small size, I recall it fondly as being more prosperous than it is now, cheerful and colorful in spring, sunny and lazy in summer, and iced with delicate frosting in winter. The view was rarely changed by human activity, the exceptions being an occasional mule and wagon grinding slowly along the roadside. Our daily interactions with people could be counted on the fingers of one hand. I realize now that a stranger would have found little charm there, and I can't imagine what city folks must have thought. But Rook was my home, and my pleasant memories of time spent catching tadpoles in ditches and honeybees buzzing among the honeysuckle vines gilded it with a beauty it probably never in fact possessed.

As there was no school in Rook, I attended the country school two miles down the road in the community of Kimble, a dismal institution for learning that served the county children. My classmates included Mr. Ryfle's son, Jesse, a dirty, ill-mannered child who glared at me during classes and taunted me at recess. All of the nine Ryfle children of school age attended the Kimble School in fits and starts, depending on the planting and harvesting schedule. The oldest, a girl named Audrey, had already graduated. Although she was three years older than I was, I had always found her to be vastly different from her savage family, and I missed seeing her at school. Willowy and graceful, Audrey was everything her father was not, and she seemed to have sprung up from another family altogether.

Being a Morton, there was a clear economic gulf between me and the other schoolchildren, but that was not what separated us. Unlike my mother, who was lively and assertive—a firecracker, Daddy used to call her—I was shy, a dreamer, wary even of those people who were familiar to me. With no shops, no theaters, no museums to attend, there was nothing for a quiet child like me to do but read. Read and imagine living in the worlds I read about, romantic moors and stately castles, places where danger and suffering were temporary and make-believe and certain to be thwarted by a strong, handsome man harboring a deep, but completely understandable, secret. In real life, I was barely able to cough out a coherent thought to a stranger, but I was adventurous in my reveries. There were no stern teachers there, no teasing schoolchildren, and no awkward adolescence to endure. But most importantly, in my fantasy world, interesting things happened.

When school began in the fall, talk of the coming enemy twittered down hallways and hijacked lessons from their course. Children stitched their own patchwork tales from snippets of theories overheard in the cotton fields and on flat-bottomed boats, or passed like pennies in the collection plate at the Kimble Baptist Church. The stories became wilder with each telling, bloodthirsty, freedom-hating Huns, desperate to steal away in the night and murder innocent Americans. Jesse Ryfle crowed of the glory of his uncles, away fighting the enemy, as if they would be single-handedly responsible for ridding the world of foreign evil.

But the day the hammers fell silent and the whine of the trucks grew fainter as they drove away from Camp Nine toward McHenry, our anxiety rose. The stillness unsettled us more than the frantic, unseen building. For when the prison was completed, the finishing touch had to be the prisoners.

Mother had spent the day at the library in Dante, twenty miles to our north, and was waiting for me when school let out. We drove toward home, the windows of the Buick rolled down as far as they would go, but the wind blowing in could not have cooled off the afternoon. The day was still sweltering even though the sun was beginning to slant slightly as the days slipped toward autumn. Along the road, thick ribbons of green plants speckled with white cotton spread before us in the fields. A loud buzz started behind us and a crop duster blew past level to the ground so that it looked like a dragonfly skimming over a pond, shooting dust out of its tail. It seemed as though it might hit the trees at the far end of the field, but I had seen these expert country pilots do their job too many times to really think that it would happen. It was still a thrill to watch them, imagining what appeared to be an inevitable crash. The fun was in knowing one would not occur. As he approached the woods, the pilot neatly completed the scene, pulling the nose straight up, and banking the plane high and to the right to make another run at the field with cotton poison.

As we rounded the bend in the highway near the store, I heard the whistle of a train, which heralded that something was amiss.

Although we owned one of the few cars in Rook, trains represented our link with the outside world, and our days were apportioned into divisions that corresponded to their arrivals and departures. In those days, highways were poor, and by the time the war had gotten into full swing, gas was rationed and limited. We rarely drove any farther than McHenry to the south or Dante to the north. But the trains were different. Whether they arrived and stopped, like the morning train from Dante which brought our mail, or sped through as if they couldn't wait to leave us, like the night train from McHenry, they were always from somewhere else and always headed yet somewhere else again. It was as if, just by stirring up the dust of our tracks, they might confer upon us some sign that we were connected with the world at large. I spent many summer nights beneath the empty skies, surrounded by lightning bugs, waiting for the red warning lights to flash and the bells to clang, just to watch the night train's glowing passenger windows fly past.

But there were no trains in the middle of the day, and yet, one was coming slowly up the tracks from the south. There was a commotion in the road ahead and Mother slowed the Buick, and then stopped it dead in the highway.

I've since seen far more military vehicles than I would ever want, but that was my first instance. The squat, dark-green jeeps blocking the road were the strangest vehicles I had ever encountered. A phalanx of soldiers milled about in the highway, young men in tan uniforms with rifles slung over their shoulders and pistols at ready in holsters on their hips. Around their arms were thick black bands with the white block letters "M.P." On the side of the highway, a soldier restrained a German shepherd tugging at its leash and pacing in the black-eyed Susans. Its companion waited placidly in the grass, bright-eyed and panting.

Our car idled at the blockade. The train rounded the corner of the woods and sounded its whistle again. It took only a moment for me to understand that it was the German prisoners of war and they were arriving in Rook that very minute.

I could tell that Mother was frightened. She said nothing, but gripped the steering wheel with her white gloves as if she were afraid that it might escape her. As the train pulled alongside us, one of the soldiers standing in the road noticed us waiting. He shifted his gun in his hands and walked our way.

The old, wooden train opposite us was unlike the sleek, silver ones that came through every morning and night. Each railcar had numbers stamped along its side, and the decrepit wheels creaked and complained as they slowed near the entrance to Camp Nine. Despite the searing heat, all of the window shades were lowered.

As the soldier approached and tipped his hat, Mother leaned her head from the window.

"Afternoon, ma'am."

"Good afternoon, sir."

He peered inside, but there was nothing to see but me, sitting in the front seat. "Sorry for the delay, ma'am, but this highway will be blocked for some time."

Mother pried her right hand from the wheel and pointed her finger past the store to our house. "I live just over there. I'm bringing my little girl home from school, and I would appreciate it if you would let us through." She pointed again to emphasize her intent. "I'm anxious to get my daughter home. She's taken ill."

I'd never known my mother to lie, and I was delighted to hear the fib slip so easily from her lips. I dug myself down into the seat and squinted my eyes to give credence to her story.

The soldier took his time looking me over. Thinking back now, I realize he was no more than eighteen or nineteen years old—a baby—and from God knows where. What had he thought of us those many years ago, that fresh-faced boy from Montana or Wyoming or Ohio, someplace where people speak flatly and without inflection? He was probably just as bewildered as I was, thrust into a strange and foreign land that existed within the borders of his own country. He discharged the duty of his pointless inspection, then straightened, and abruptly left to confer with his colleagues.

The train, now stopped, sounded its whistle twice, and at that, all of the window shades opened at the same time. Startled, I sat up straight, craning to look. I'd never before seen either a German or a prisoner, and I was anxious to see both at once. Emboldened by the safety of our car, I hoped secretly that some ragged and disgraced enemy of freedom might make a mad dash to escape, just so I would see how fast the dogs could run.

A face appeared in the train window opposite my car door, close enough almost to touch. But it wasn't a German soldier. It was only a child, younger even than I. In that brief moment that it took me to realize that she looked Chinese, the windows filled with what appeared to be Chinese families, mothers, fathers, and children, packed tightly into the train, tired and worried, all fighting for the chance to look out the window at our Buick and our house and our little town.

And me.

They looked without speaking, wide-eyed, at the tall grass growing alongside the track and the sign that sprouted from it that announced their destination: "Rook, pop. 86."

Mother's hands slipped from the wheel. Her eyes narrowed and her mouth assumed the position of words, but none came.

The soldier had returned and was talking to her through the open window.

"Ma'am?" he repeated.

"Yes. Yes," she said, swiveling toward him.

A jeep's engine started up. It pulled off the highway, opening our path.

"You can go on, but only as far as your home, please." The soldier touched the tip of his cap with his fingertips.

Mother put the car in gear. "Thank you," she said, but she neglected to touch the gas.

The soldier started away.

Mother called after him. "Sir?"

He walked back, shading his eyes against the afternoon sun, and leaned into the car. "Where are the Germans?" she asked.

He glanced at the train. "Not Germans, ma'am. These are Japanese. From California." He stood straight and touched his cap again. "Drive careful, now."

As he walked away, Mother called after him. "But . . ."

He turned briefly and waved. "That's all I can tell you, ma'am." We watched his back as he rejoined his companions.

I didn't know why they had come. Could entire families be enemy agents, right down to the smallest of children held in their mothers' arms? A different kind of trouble settled over me. A girl, my age, in a red vest and white shirt, tugged at a strand of her hair and worried her tongue inside her mouth. I felt childish, selfish fears, but it was all happening so fast all I could do was try to understand it in the context of what it meant to me.

Mother took one last look at the train beside our car, then pulled slowly down the highway through the blockade. As we made the corner to the house, I turned in my seat. Just before I lost sight of the faces in the train, my eyes locked on a boy with peanut butter skin and black pepper eyes, so handsome and so bewildered. I lifted my hand to wave, but he looked through me as though none of this was really happening. This was an expression I would see in David Matsui's eyes many times over the coming months. It was as if he had convinced himself that if he could not see what was happening to him, to his family, then it must not be true.

Chapter 2

Through the brilliant changes of autumn and the colorless slush of winter, the trains continued to arrive, bearing Japanese families from California. Without warning, jeeps and trucks would appear and block the highway, and a rickety wooden train would groan and slow to a stop at the station. Waves of people, shocked and disoriented, would disembark and mill about in a daze until they were rounded up into trucks like so many sheep and goats and taken across the tracks away from our sight. We received no communications from the military, but from the very first day, we understood that the Japanese would be isolated, separated from the rest of us by fences topped with barbed wire, and manned and armed towers. But mostly, we separated ourselves from them, by refusing to acknowledge they were even there.

Finally, the trains and trucks stopped altogether and it became quiet again, the kind of quiet that should have been peaceful, but it wasn't normal. By then, Rook was a tiny root from which grew a mushroom of a city behind walls. Other than the thick tracks of mud that stretched onto the highway from vehicles leaving Camp Nine and the curls of dim smoke coming from the smokestack, we could see no evidence of activity, and most people conducted their lives as if there weren't ten thousand people a stone's throw away behind the barbed wire. Even at school, on the rare occasion someone mentioned Camp Nine, our teacher snapped at us to keep our minds on our own business.

I was as guilty as everyone else in my desire to pretend nothing was happening at Camp Nine, and with my first sight of an autumn leaf in October, I welcomed the thoughts of Christmas vacation that began creeping into my head. The reedy, echoing sound of a woodpecker indicated the thinning of the air that foretold coming holidays even before the landscape changed. These sights and sounds primed me to drift away from my lessons, down deep into a fantasy of the boxes Mother kept up the dark stairs in our gloomy attic, which was illuminated by a solitary four-paned window through which light barely filtered. While my teacher deadened my reality by scratching fractions on the chalkboard, my mind climbed the stairs with anticipation, searching among the dusty cardboard boxes stuffed with satin Halloween costumes, baby toys, and clothes since discarded, until I found the holy grail of the season—the glittery glass ornaments and velvet skirt for our tree.

It seemed to snow more then than now, and, too young to appreciate the difficulty that accompanied the occasional dumping of heavy snow, I was always enchanted by it. Along with a welcome snowfall, Christmas was a time for special treats, like the multi-colored iced molasses cookies baked each morning by Mrs. Capps down the road and the oranges Mother ordered for me from New Orleans.

Just when it seemed that I could hold no more tension and that I would burst if required to wait one more day, the time arrived. School was to let out that afternoon and not resume until January. To top off my delight, that morning Mr. Gilwell had called to say the oranges had arrived.

Riding down Highway 1 away from the Kimble School, I was so free I felt as though we were flying. We reached the gravel lot of Mr. Gilwell's store and parked underneath the wooden water tower. At the depot, across the highway, a dark train sat on the tracks. A soldier stood on the platform, stamping his feet, and patting his thick, wool sleeves with his hands. Though the entrance to Camp Nine was within our sight, we no longer saw military men, and although we spied a solitary jeep on occasion, how the soldiers and other personnel came and went was a mystery to me. The entire enterprise was conducted in such secret, it was as though they landed and departed in spaceships while we slept.

Mother touched my arm to break my lingering look at the strange sight of the soldier and ushered me up the worn, wooden steps into the store, where a potbellied stove glowed in the corner.

Mr. Gilwell's mercantile, the original plantation store, looms larger in my memory than I'm sure it actually was, that same stove overheating one March morning the year I left for college, burning the building to the ground to be replaced with a more modern structure. Inside the door on the left were canned and boxed goods, and on the right, fabrics and notions and a long table with a measuring tape running its length. The counter and cash register were in the middle, stacked high with brightly colored boxes of candy and glass cylinders holding cookies. A pickle barrel occupied a great deal of space on the floor. In the summer, a gigantic ceiling fan fretted and complained overhead.

A flight of stairs led to a balcony where Mr. Gilwell outfitted the black farm workers with cotton duck and denim clothing. Although there was no sign limiting access to whites, it was understood that no proper white person other than Mr. Gilwell would go upstairs. It was in that separate area that the personal necessities of black people were tended to, and it was therefore an unsuitable area for whites. Other than the infrequent smattering of muted voices and the shuffling of boots overhead, the balcony was as quiet and guarded as a tomb.

In the back was the town's combination post office and telegraph station. Mr. Gilwell manned both, and so was always the first to receive information coming into town and the one to relay the occasional snippet of local news to the world outside.

Mother's dark-green swing coat moved smoothly from side to side with each step she made toward the post office. Mr. Gilwell balanced several stamped envelopes between his fingers, peering through thick lenses at the writing on them. "Your oranges come in on the train yesterday, Carrie," he said, recognizing her by the sound of her shoes. "I got 'em in the storage shed, keeping cool. Give me a second to finish sorting this mail and I'll go get 'em."

"I've waited all year," Mother said with a smile. "I expect I can wait a couple more minutes." She laid her gloves over in her hand and turned her back on him to demonstrate her patience, a necessary virtue for our slow country life.

Mr. Gilwell slid a stack of letters into the *A*-through-*C* slot in the board behind him.

"Is that a private railcar outside?" Mother asked.

Mr. Gilwell thrust another stack of envelopes in the *D*-through-*F* slot. "Army," he said.

"Beg pardon?"

"Army," he repeated. "Some big shot from Camp Shelby visiting Camp Nine. I took a telegram out there to the superintendent this morning."

"Ah," Mother said, raising her eyebrows. "Must be something going on."

"Must be," he said. It was a simple reply that signified there was nothing left to discuss. We waited politely, pretending to be interested in objects we'd seen a hundred times before.

"Gibbons boys left McHenry yesterday," Mr. Gilwell said, fulfilling his role as town crier.

Mother had already heard that bit of news, but it was custom to feign surprise and permit the speaker the joy of believing he'd relayed useful and astonishing information. "You don't say," she said. "Both of them?"

"One navy, one army," he said, stuffing several letters into the *W*-through-*Z* slot.

"How many's that enlisted now?" she asked.

"Oh, ten at least, not counting the colored boys. I don't know how many of them there is gone off. Hammond Ryfle laid hands on the white ones over to Kimble Baptist last Sunday."

Mother was incredulous. "Hammond Ryfle?"

It seemed that Brother Akin, the ordained minister of the Kimble Baptist Church and a relative moderate under the circumstances, had lost the fire of his congregation. It was a fact that Mother would not have known, as the matter had been somewhat swept under the rug and was not freely discussed except among fellow disgruntled Baptists, which, apparently, was most of them. Mr. Ryfle, an appointed deacon, had stirred the pot of the brimstone, which the congregation desired, and had risen to the top, taking his place at the head of the committee seeking to limit Brother Akin's influence.

"Can Hammond Ryfle even read?" Mother asked, even though she recognized that it was an insulting exaggeration. She'd seen his shaky scrawl on an assortment of required agricultural forms, and knew he had at least a rudimentary grasp of reading and writing.

Mr. Gilwell laughed. "The Bible? Yes. A newspaper? No." He launched a single, final letter into a slot like a torpedo, and stepped from behind his postman's cage. "I'll go get your oranges now," he said, turning a corner toward the back of the store and warbling on his way out to a storage shed. Encounters with Mother always seemed to brighten his day.

Mother wound her way through the aisles toward the fabrics at the edge of the store, stopping to admire a bolt of purple-printed cotton corduroy and running her fingers over the rows. "Isn't this pretty, Chess?" she said.

At the creak of the screen door, a shock of cold air flooded the room, and three soldiers entered the store. They shook the frost from their shoulders and surveyed the dimly lit space.

An officer in a heavy coat strode purposefully behind them. The line of his jaw was softened by a cashmere scarf knotted beneath his collar, and the flush of his cheeks set off his pale eyes. As he passed me, he removed his hat and ran his hand through his close cropped hair. The scent of his aftershave moved a moment behind him. To this day, it recalls itself to me in unguarded moments.

Mr. Gilwell appeared through the back door, lugging a burlap bag, stopping short when he saw the strangers. He set the bag gently on the floor and stood up straight, drawing himself to his full height.

"Good afternoon," the officer said.

"Good afternoon, Colonel," Mr. Gilwell replied.

"I was wondering if I might use your telephone to call Camp Nine. Our train was a bit early."

"Yessir," Mr. Gilwell said, scurrying to the receiver and handing it to the colonel. "Help yourself. Dial four one."

The colonel stuffed his gloves in the pocket of his overcoat. A single pleat cut the wool into two halves that fell all the way to his calves.

"Yes," he said, "this is Tom Jefferies from Camp Shelby."

I knew at once by Mother's reaction that Tom Jefferies was not a stranger to her. She teetered for a moment as if she might topple then turned in what seemed to be slow motion.

Tom Jefferies paused, listening to the voice on the other side. "We're up at the mercantile," he said, shifting his weight. "Fine, we'll be here." He replaced the receiver.

Mother stood in the shadow of the faint light filtering through the door, the color drained from her face, staring at Tom Jefferies as though he were an object she'd suddenly remembered from long ago. When she finally spoke, it was only a soft peep like the sound of a tiny bird. "Tom?"

He looked up, uncertain from where the voice had come. A look of recognition lit his features. "Carolina March?"

The sky had changed. It still snowed gently as we walked, Mother, Tom, and I, to the car, and the clouds pressed down on us, just as before. But there was a radiance to the sky, a sense that although every physical thing seemed the same, the earth had turned on its axis, and we were now on the other side of where we had been moments before. I climbed into the passenger seat as the soldier with the oranges, now an afterthought, opened the trunk of the car, put the burlap bag inside, and set off back toward the store.

Tom opened Mother's door and leaned on it, pushing the brim of his hat back away from his forehead. A wispy wet flake of snow glided into the felt of his overcoat and stuck. Another fell onto his cheekbone and melted on his skin.

Mother looked into his face for a moment, then gathered up her pocketbook into both gloved hands, and slid into the driver's side. "Tom," she said, formally, "this is my daughter, Cecilia. Everyone calls her 'Chess.'"

His startling eyes were fully focused on me now. "After your great-grandmother," he said. That a man I had just met knew such intimate details about me made me wonder what else he knew about our lives. "I'm pleased to meet you, Chess."

I was speechless in the face of his powerful gaze, searching my features as if he were looking for something specific. "Thank you," I murmured.

Mother closed the car door and rolled down the window.

He pressed toward her slightly. "How's Walt?"

She hesitated. "Walt passed away. Some time ago."

Hearing Mother inform someone of Daddy's death was sad and strange. Everyone who had any need to know had learned of it immediately. The fact of his passing was so central to who we were that I couldn't imagine that there was anyone in the world who knew her, and yet didn't know he was gone.

He put his hands on the inside of the car and leaned in. "I'm sorry, Carrie. I really am." He inched closer, his hand slipping farther down the inside of the car door.

She intercepted his fingers with hers. "Thank you," she said.

It was the first of a thousand times I would see the thin gold band around his finger. Why I even focused on such a thing, I don't recall. But it stood out against the bland upholstery of our car and the smooth, tapered flesh of his fingers, and it tapped against the inside of the car door as she patted the back of his hand. For a moment, they were at a loss for words.

"I'm at Camp Nine for the night," he said finally. "I'm heading back to Mississippi tomorrow afternoon."

She dropped her hands into her lap and trained her eyes on them. "Would you like to have supper with us tonight?"

"I'd like that," he said.

Some days, the quiet got to Mother.

A talented artist and voracious student, she'd left Rook before she'd even graduated from high school on a scholarship to a state university in California. Her tales of her travels made me think it was bold and grand of her to take the train alone across country to an unfamiliar land. But then, Mother was the adventurous one. Now that I have children of my own, and I see how different they are from each other—one shy and cautious, the other animated and fearless—I often wonder what it would have been like to have had a sister and whether she would have been more like Mother than I was. I could only observe Mother's gaiety and charm with awe and envy.

But back in Rook, there were no exciting adventures for her. Mother's stories of her life before me sounded as though they were things that had happened to someone else. Ruby Jean said that Mother was wasting away not having anything to do that made her feel useful. I countered that she had plenty to do with taking care of our house and sewing all my clothes, but Ruby Jean said that was just busy work and that what she was talking about was different.

Ruby Jean's insight was lost on me, wrapped as it was in riddles. I didn't know what she was talking about half the time. The convention of our day and region dictated that we live in a social contradiction of familiarity and distance. She could never come right out and say what she really meant about any of us. The rigidity of societal norms was as much a part of the landscape as the river itself. The arrangement suited me, but I now wonder how she and her kin managed such stricture.

With nowhere to focus her energy, there were days when Mother's restlessness floated through our small house, stiff and unpleasant, like the smell of Ruby Jean's starch. I learned to anticipate the moment when she would sail past me, out the door to the carport, keys already in hand, and ask if I'd like to accompany her on a drive. It was a scene familiar to us both, and our parts were memorized from repetition.

Her escape route varied. Sometimes we took Highway 1 toward McHenry, turning off to drive along the open and airy Amos Lake, a cheerful drive where she might chatter about pleasant things, plans she had to farm progressive new crops like sunflowers, plans that were entirely dependent on Mr. Ryfle's availability, and, therefore, never realized. If she were in the mood to sing, she might turn on the radio, and we would drive all the way to Dante, hearing the newest songs by Glenn Miller, Lionel Hampton, or our favorite, Jimmy Dorsey, and visit the soda shop there for a milkshake and a grilled cheese sandwich.

On sorrowful days, it was Rook Lane to the levee road.

Rook Lane, a narrow, dusty road leading to the levee, passed between dense rows of cypress trees and emerged into the middle of the fields where our tenant farmers lived, all related to Ruby Jean. Their shacks, just down the road from where Mother's unpainted house had once stood, were little gray squares that lined up in a row, and reminded me of the houses on my Monopoly board. They backed up along Black Bayou with only a dirt track linking them. In the winter, smoke curled out of their chimneys, and in the summer, sheets and pillowcases and men's shirts and women's dresses hung from the wash lines like white flags hanging limp in the damp air.

Ruby Jean lived in the one farthest back. Next to hers were the homes of our field hands, Homer and Cecil, and finally the fourth, belonging to Ruby Jean's uncle, Willie Monroe. Willie was blind and had been from birth. He was an enigmatic figure to me, doted on and segregated by Ruby Jean in equal parts. His misfortune was a fascination. When pressed, Ruby Jean would lapse into a singsong voice and recount, as if it were a fable of epic consequence, that Willie's mother had been caught up in a raging epidemic of yellow fever when she was expecting him, and that he'd never seen the light of day. She always concluded the sad tale with her verdict that the Good Lord doesn't take but what He gives back double, and that was why Willie could play the guitar and sound like two men playing it at one time. Part of Willie's allure, in the rare times I was in his presence, was that though I could witness the fever's devastation to his eyes, I was not permitted to hear his gift. Such was Ruby Jean's power to control the interaction between us.

Ruby Jean let slip once something of such mystifying appeal that I never forgot it. Willie was known county-wide as "Cottonmouth Monroe." I don't believe she'd intended me to know it, but once she'd told me, she allowed proudly that the reason was, aside from his musical gifts, Willie was a born snake conjurer. There were people, she said, of such extraordinary grace that even the serpents bent to their will. Willie's skill was so widely regarded that, in his day, he'd been called by many a farmwife to rid their grounds of infestations of moccasins, which were social reptiles and preferred to migrate in extended family groups like gypsies.

Past the tenant shacks, the levee rose like an emerald mountain, and the Mississippi River, invisible on the other side, was even larger in my imagination. At the time, I didn't appreciate how deeply the levee influenced our lives. Massive and splendid, it seemed to be alive, a colossal creature coiled beside us. The gravel road rose up into the sky to a flat dirt path that ran along the top. On one side were trees, trees, and more trees, wild, crazy, black things as tall as one could see with great green vines covering all the branches. Between the levee and the woods were the bar pits, the ditches and ponds left over from when working crews carved the earth to build the levee. Odessa had mesmerized me one entire winter afternoon with her memory of the days of the levee building, when whole cities of black men lived there in a string of work camps, numbered one to ten. Camp Nine got its name that way, for being nearly the end of the line of them. It was something that I couldn't imagine, for they were then all gone; any evidence of them vanished into the wilderness.

Down below were the cultivated fields. Occasionally, the house of a levee family would appear in a rough clearing, a little shack with a cow or two and sometimes horses, although more often a couple of mules. At every such home, chickens roamed the yard and scrawny dogs napped in the swept yards underneath shade trees. Some of the houses were built atop Indian burial mounds that predated modern settlement.

There had once been mounds on the Morton Plantation, but Grandpa had them bulldozed to the ground to make the fields level to grow cotton and soybeans. Years before, when my father had bought Camp Nine and Mr. Ryfle had leveled out the mound there, Ruby Jean took Willie and me on a picnic. I found some Spanish coins and a gold cross, which I kept in the cedarwood treasure box that Mother received as a gift on her wedding day.

Mr. Gilwell offered to buy them from me, but Mother talked me into keeping them. She said things get more valuable the longer you keep them, and that I shouldn't part with them until I found something so special that I was willing to trade my treasures just to get it. That summer, there was nothing in the world I wanted more than my Spanish gold. At night before sleep, I would take the pieces out and turn them over and over in my fingers and imagine that they were carried by Hernando DeSoto himself. I closed my eyes and tried to picture what Arkansas was like when Spanish explorers ran through the woods and Indians lived nearby. The Kimble School taught us nothing that happened in Arkansas before the Civil War. To me, those coins were proof of another time.

On the best drives, I was treated to Mother's stories about the life she had before she married Daddy and settled back into life in the Delta, of days at the red brick college in California where she wore cloche hats and silk stockings and studied painting and design. I could go with her while she danced again at parties in San Francisco and bought flowers at Union Square and ate food that she didn't know how to pronounce in Chinatown.

Out back, there was an arch that rose over our driveway and announced the backside of the Morton Plantation. On past the arch, across the big, broad pasture where Daddy once kept our horses, there was a barn where Mother used to paint when the weather was pleasant. I recall lying on my back on one of Ruby Jean's quilts in the middle of the straw, among the canvasses and bottles of all colors of paint, watching the muscles in Mother's back move and ripple as she pulled a brush across the white surface of the canvas. Sometimes she'd pick up a small brush and whisk tiny strokes in places. She'd sit so long she would occasionally stop and stretch, but I lay still. Daddy would creep quietly through the open door, casting a shadow across my eyes. Saying nothing, he would stand behind her and pull her hair up into a loose bundle, holding it while he watched her paint. He would let it fall as he turned to go in for his bath before supper.

After Daddy died, she no longer painted. For years, the barn had been locked. And by then, Mother had taken to letting Ruby Jean go home early every night, and she cooked supper for just the two of us.

Chapter 3

Although she tried to hide it, it was clear that our chance encounter with Tom Jefferies had deeply affected Mother. She underwent an immediate shift in mood, leaving the oranges in the trunk and sailing into the kitchen, where Ruby Jean was pulling a chicken from the ice box.

"No chicken tonight, Ruby Jean!"

Ruby Jean blinked in surprise. "What you gone eat?" she asked.

Mother dropped her pocketbook on the counter and slid the coat from her arms in one fluid movement, as if she were discarding a dancing partner and freeing herself to embrace another. "I'm going to go pick up some of that aged beef from Mr. Carter." She slipped an apron over her dress and tied it behind her back.

Ruby Jean knitted her brows and peered at Mother as if she'd lost her mind. "Aged beef? You gonna use coupons in the middle of the week?" Strict wartime rationing had reduced us to limiting beef to special occasions.

Mother grasped Ruby Jean by her sleeve. "We have an army officer coming for dinner tonight."

Ruby Jean shook her free and grumbled. "Ain't no cause to use no coupons. You ain't got but a few left."

Mother opened the ice box and leaned into it. "Oh, you'll change your tune, Ruby Jean. You will, you'll see. 'Course," Mother said loudly, her head in the ice box, "I don't have a thing for dessert."

Seeing Mother in such a playful mood was an unexpected treat. But she loved to bait Ruby Jean, and she knew exactly how to do it. "I raised you better than to have company with no dessert, Miss Carrie."

Mother closed the ice box. "Oh, we'll make do," she said airily. "It's only Tom Jefferies. He won't know any better."

The mention of Tom's name took a moment to sink in, but when it did, Ruby Jean thrust her head forward in surprise, then set her jaw firmly. "Tom Jefferies? I thought we was all done with that man."

Mother's eyes darted furtively in my direction, and her voice took on the tone of some formality. "Ruby Jean, he's away from home, over at Camp Nine. I just want to be hospitable."

Ruby Jean muttered under her breath, a habit she had to indicate her disagreement about something she knew she had no say in. But the spring in her step belied her complaints. Whatever Tom had done, she could not hide that she would not hold it against him for long. "You don't know company from a hole in the ground," she grumbled, pulling a clean apron from a drawer. "Tom Jefferies's eaten my cooking long enough to know better, too. I'm gone get you a pie going before you embarrass yourself. You better get on over to Dante 'fore Mr. Carter close."

The fact that now, not just Mother, but also Ruby Jean, knew this strange man who it seemed had fallen suddenly from the sky into our lives deepened his mystery. But up to their elbows in flour and sugar, they said no more about him, so I left them in the kitchen to play their affectionate parts, and headed into the tiny addition on the side of our house that had once been my father's old study.

The room had been our favorite place to spend time together when we weren't riding in his truck or on our horses. I recall him sitting at the desk underneath a crackled glass lamp, crouching over a fly-tying clamp, tying bits of horsehair and feathers around a fish hook. The contraption was long gone, but I still loved the lamp and the desk and the chair that remained.

I gathered memories of him in secret, careful not to pain Mother with his mention, but anxious that he not disappear forever. How she coped with his loss, I don't know, for we almost never spoke of him. It was odd that although she shared so much with me, her only companion, the subject of my own father was strangely, albeit tacitly, off-limits, and her relationship with Grandma and Grandpa was so strained it seemed impossible that he could have been loved by them and by her at the same time. The answer must have been his easy nature, a gift Mother did not have. While her assessments of people were carefully and justly made, once she formed a low opinion of someone, she found it hard not to maintain it. When I pressed Ruby Jean for memories of Daddy, her first words were always that he never knew a stranger.

I sank into his oversized leather chair and spent the next three hours in the romantic English countryside with Jane Eyre, holding at bay the crushing boredom of the Arkansas Delta. Although dinner time was not yet near, the door opened and Mother appeared. "Have you had your bath, Chess?"

I barely looked up. "No ma'am."

But her appearance caught my attention. She looked more beautiful than I'd seen her in years, dressed in an emerald-green silk she'd pulled from the back of her closet. Around her throat was a sparkling jewel necklace I'd not even known she had. "For heaven's sake," she said, flipping the switch on the overhead light, "you're going to put your eyes out trying to read by that dim lamp. Colonel Jefferies is coming for dinner, and I'd like you to be dressed and ready when he gets here. Now come on!"

I hopped up and walked past her, the bright lights of the dining room flashing off the shiny things she usually kept hidden in the cabinets. She'd set the table with her good china and crystal, and filled a glass bowl with oranges set atop a pale-green cloth. Once a month, Ruby Jean would take out the silver to polish it, but we never actually ate with it, and yet, there it was on the table, placed alongside the china we never used.

I went down the hall to the bathroom, put the stopper in the tub, and turned on the tap. There was so much energy in the house that night, it felt as though Christmas had already arrived. I stood before my closet imagining what it would be like to have that feeling all of the time.

That night, when Tom came, we enjoyed an elaborate meal that surpassed all others in my memory. There passed between Mother and Tom lively discussions concerning the progress of the war, the current state of America's agricultural system, and the relative merits of train travel versus the new and exciting air travel, which Tom felt certain would supplant rail in the near future. But aside from the fact that Tom was married and that he and his wife were now the proud parents of three young girls, I learned nothing more of who he was or how he knew us. He had known Ruby Jean and Mother's father, Giorgio, and he expressed his sorrow when Mother told him that Giorgio had died. That he had not known that told me that they'd not been in touch for some time, for Giorgio had died shortly before Mother and Daddy married.

Toward the end of our meal, there was more time between bites. The silver forks clinked less often against the china, and the conversation slowed and fell into a quieter rhythm. A candle's flame reflected off Mother's jeweled necklace as she kept the conversation on general topics. Sitting at the head of the table, she glowed like a candle herself.

It was already past my usual bedtime, and though I would have loved to have stayed, my time with them drew to an end. Mother folded her napkin and placed it aside her dessert plate. "Chess," she said, "it's about time for you to be getting on to bed."

"Yes, ma'am," I said, sliding from my chair.

Tom's chair was pushed back away from the table, and his shirt sleeves were rolled, revealing the round veins in his arm. The muscles in his jaw contracted and then relaxed as he leaned back, crossing his left ankle over his right knee. His jacket hung on the back of the empty chair beside him. "Goodnight, Chess," he said. "I hope that you have pleasant dreams."

"'Night, Mama. 'Night, Colonel Jefferies." I separated myself from them and walked the carpet strip down the hallway. I waited a moment, then peeked around the corner to steal one last look at them sharing an awkward moment.

I trudged down the hallway and into my bedroom, and carefully hung my dress on a hanger in the closet, clinging to it for a moment as if I could make the night last longer. Slipping into bed, I pulled one of Ruby Jean's quilts around my chin and listened to the unfamiliar sound of a guest in our home. I lay quietly and drank it in, trying to memorize the feeling.

Echoes bounced through walls as Mother and Tom left the dining room and settled into the living room. The radio came on, and as the voice of the announcer floated through the house, Mother's laughter sparkled like a Christmas ornament against Tom's low velvet tone.

A chorus of muted trumpets rose and fell, the beginning strains of a Benny Goodman song. A smooth clarinet played the melody. I sang the words to myself before Helen Ward sang them on the radio.

Deep sadness settled into a hollow space in my chest I hadn't known was there. I had been so comfortable within the cocoon of our daily habits, I'd not noticed that something had been missing. I slid quietly from the bed, crept into the hall, and crouched at the edge of the living room, my knees drawn up, my arms linked across them. The lamps were turned down low, and the fire glowed in orange waves against the wall. The fat red, green, and blue Christmas lights looked like electric fruit roped around the tree.

Mother sat on the couch, her feet tucked underneath her. Across from her, Tom sank back in an upholstered chair. The colored lights shone through the ice in the highball glass he held in his hand. He had loosened his tie, and his face formed sharp, hard angles in the flickering light.

"I would tell you if it weren't classified," he said.

"I was just so surprised when they arrived," she said. "No one told us anything about it."

"One day, you'd be hard-pressed to find fifty people in this little town," he said, "and the next thing you know, it's one of the biggest cities in Arkansas."

"And all the residents are from California," she said, laughing. "But why, Tom? I know the details are classified, but surely you can tell me that much."

Tom's response was slow in coming and began with the government's official policy: the Japanese on the West Coast were a security risk. With their tight ties to family and to Japan, there was no way of knowing who might betray us. The secretary of the navy had even testified that spies in Honolulu had guided the bombing of Pearl Harbor. It wasn't true, but it had helped deflect criticism directed at him for being unprepared for an attack he should have known was coming.

Besides the danger to America from the Japanese, there was the safety of the innocent Japanese themselves to consider. Long a target of hostile whites on the West Coast, the argument was that they were better off in isolated regions, where they would be safe from misguided retribution.

But as they spoke, and under pressing questions from Mother, Tom admitted that those reasons were false. None of them, together or alone, was justification for what had happened. The real reason, Tom believed, was greed. With their serious work ethic and their sharp business acumen, the Japanese were fierce economic competitors with the white community. By the time of the war, the vast majority of California's lucrative vegetable trade was controlled by Japanese farmers. If their businesses were to be closed, well, then the wartime boom in business was there for the taking.

Mother sat quietly, absorbing the information. "But they're going back after the war, right?"

Tom shrugged. "Who knows if there will be anything left for them after the war?"

There was a pause in the conversation, then Tom raised his glass and the light scattered. "Enough of this serious talk. How did you like California?"

"Oh, I liked it fine," Mother said softly, lifting sections of her hair and raking her fingers through it. "The weather was beautiful. There were restaurants. Parties. Seems like a long time ago, now. And it's so strange that this has happened. Some of my friends there were Japanese."

He shifted in his chair, leaning forward so that his elbows rested on his knees. "Carrie," he said, staring into his glass.

She lifted her hand. "Don't, Tom."

"Did you get my letters?" he asked.

"Yes," she said, so quietly I wasn't sure she actually said it.

"Why didn't you answer?"

"What good would it have done? You married Maxine. There was a new life waiting for me, and I took it."

It had never occurred to me to question the stories she told of her life before. They were fairy tales, fantasies in which everyone was good and kind, and life was gay and exciting. That she had come back to Arkansas and married my father was just the logical end to the story. I'd not considered there could have been other endings.

When she told him that Daddy had supported her during Giorgio's long illness, and that when she was ready to return to California, Daddy himself had fallen ill, I felt a disquiet run through me, as if she'd been hiding something from me my entire life.

I'm sure it was a miracle that I had ever been born. Mother had sacrificed her future to marry a dying man out of obligation. No sensible couple would have planned a child. But even now, I remember their affection for each other during his long, taxing illnesses, and I was there to witness her genuine grief when it was finally all over. I can't bring myself to believe there wasn't something more.

"What's here for you?" Tom asked, his eyes taking in our living room. "Look at yourself. You're young. You're beautiful. You're educated."

"I also have a daughter," she said sharply. "And this is her home."

"Carrie, I'm sorry, I shouldn't question you."

"I loved Walt very much," she said. "I was happy to come here with him. And when he died, I was happy to stay here. There's a piece of him here." She paused, then forced a laugh and fanned her fingers so that her ruby ring sparkled. "Listen to us both being silly. 'Of all the sad words of tongue or pen,' right?"

The wall clock chimed to sound the hour. "You're right," Tom said. "What's happened has happened." He set his glass on the end table and straightened his tie. "I should go. I need to be getting on back to Camp Nine."

The Benny Goodman band played the last refrain. Mother unfolded her legs and slipped her feet into her shoes. She rose as he lifted his jacket from the chair and crossed the room to her. He seemed poised to reach for her, but she remained awkwardly still.

"Thank you for dinner," he said.

"I didn't do anything special," she said brightly. "Chess and I had to eat, didn't we?" She studied her hands, then smiled at him gamely. "It was wonderful to see you again, Tom. I'm just amazed to have run into you like this."

The announcer spoke animatedly of Lucky Strike cigarettes. Tom moved closer to Mother, then hesitated. She thrust out her hand to him, and after a brief moment, he clasped it warmly and shook it.

She walked to the front door, chose his overcoat from the coat-rack, and handed it to him. He slipped it over his uniform, then pulled his gloves from the pockets. "You should come out to Camp Nine with me tomorrow," he said. "We built a bunch of barracks, but the Japanese have built a city. They've got a school and a newspaper. They're even putting together a Boy Scout troop. They're going to rise above this."

She shook her head. "I don't know, Tom."

He put his hands on her shoulders. "Please, Carrie. Come see for yourself what's there."

She lightly shrugged. "I'll come out in the morning. Just to see you off."

Violins opened "White Christmas" and Bing Crosby's voice covered the room liked melted chocolate. Tom leaned into Mother and kissed her cheek. "Goodnight, Carrie."

The front door closed. I made my way quietly to bed and waited on her to come to me. But she didn't. Dishes were rattled about. Eventually, the radio shut off and I heard the sound of her footsteps pad down the hall. As I drifted off to sleep, I thought I heard her crying softly, which was a sound I hadn't heard come from her room in a very long time.

Chapter 4

Ruby Jean blamed the nearly constant snow on the Germans. She claimed it had never snowed that much in DeSoto County and insisted they'd sprayed the world with some kind of mustard gas that was making the weather change. Mother told her that they didn't use mustard gas any more, but Ruby Jean just shook her head and said that, whatever it was they were using now, it must be worse than mustard gas.

Two weeks after our supper with Tom, the night before Christmas Eve, the snow turned to ice, which fell like rain but collected on the roads and the trees in great, heavy sheets. By the next evening, the forecast was for better weather, but it was too late to save Christmas Day. We'd be homebound, unable to attend Mass at the Catholic church in McHenry.

Although we lived next door to them and saw them often, I was not comfortable with my grandparents. In fact, I was terrified of them. My grandmother, Agnes Heston Morton, dressed in tweeds and furs, a single strand of pearls a constant fixture around her neck. Educated at convent school, Grandma was a model of respectability and reserve, and I sensed her disappointment in me with each encounter. She was fonder of my only cousin, Mary Grace, whom everyone called Babe, a blonde doll with porcelain skin and cornflower-blue eyes. My clothes were in constant disarray from outdoor play, my hair and skin smelled like fresh air, and my introversion caused all the right words to be found ten to twenty minutes after they'd been called for and the need for them had already passed. Grandma admonished Mother not to allow me so much sun, but no amount of shade could disguise my Mediterranean heritage, which must have been an embarrassment to her. I can now only imagine the force of the resistance my father had surely met in marrying Mother in the first place. It tells me something, all these years later, about his own integrity that he managed to wed her at all.

Grandpa was another matter. Scrappy and ambitious, he was quick with the joke told without real humor—always at the expense of someone else. I feared constantly that I would be a direct target, so I spent my time around him making myself as inconspicuous as possible, just in case he, like Grandma, found me lacking in one or another matter they found desirable.

Late on Christmas Eve, the fireplace in the den of the big house was a crackling inferno. We were enduring our Christmas visit, a formality that had attached to it no emotion that one would associate with the happiness of the season. In short, it was a chore, but at least we got our obligations out of the way on Christmas Eve and were spared Christmas Day when my Aunt Margaret would arrive with Babe and Margaret's hapless dishrag of a husband, Harold.

Grandma sat erect, hand-stitching lace. Grandpa reclined in his leather easy chair, a detective magazine in his hands, the flames reflecting in his round glasses. Mother read a mystery novel in a stuffed chair, her legs crossed. The grandfather clock in the corner ticked.

Grandma stirred and made the muffled coughing sound that was her way of starting a conversation, then she batted her face with a handkerchief and looked at the clock. "It's nearly nine," she said.

Mother rearranged her knees. "Where did the time go?"

Grandma pulled a velvet curtain from the window. Against the glow cast by the porch light, fat white flakes were falling fast. "I don't suppose we'll make it to Mass tonight. Or in the morning."

"Why don't you just come with us tomorrow, Agnes?" Mother asked.

An expression of disapproval floated across Grandma's brow.

"It's a regular priest from Los Angeles," Mother continued. "A Maryknoller. Besides, it's not like you to miss Mass."

Grandma's thin lips drew together. "I don't understand half the things you do, Carrie."

The starchy magazine pages grated together as Grandpa turned to the next sensational story. "Don't go sticking your nose where it doesn't belong, Mrs. Morton," he said from behind a cartoon picture of a half-dressed woman in distress.

Grandma directed her pointed face at Mother. "People are starting to talk about your comings and goings."

"Come now, Agnes," Mother said, "I know you're above that sort of idle gossip."

Grandma poked at the lace with a silver needle. "My behavior isn't the subject of the complaint."

I pretended to be transfixed by the Christmas tree. Honest confrontation was not in Grandma's nature, a trait which I inherited from her and which I still deplore. And although my mother would normally have argued with a barn door, in dealings with my grandparents, she would observe the decorum of their home. All of us knew what Grandma was alluding to. Since Tom's visit, Mother had been to Camp Nine, not just that once, but often. She'd tried to draw me into conversations about it, but, like the David I would soon come to know, I believed that if I wished something away, it couldn't be real. The less I knew about Camp Nine and its place in her world, the better. And I wasn't alone. By those in the community who were willing to accept their presence, Camp Nine and its inhabitants, out of sight, away over the tracks, were a danger to be tolerated. But not embraced. Those people were foreigners here, and they were not welcome.

Mother rose. "The offer is still there if you change your mind. Chess and I are going in the morning." She leaned into Grandma and pecked her lips against Grandma's cheek, leaving a faint red streak against the fine pale powder. "Goodnight, Agnes. Goodnight, Walter."

My pulse quickened. Somewhere in my mind I must have known she wouldn't let me avoid Camp Nine forever, that she felt it was important that I see things for myself. I suppose I simply hoped I would have had more warning.

"'Night, Carrie," Grandpa grumbled.

We crossed the threshold into the hallway, and Grandma came behind us to hold the back door open. "Chess," she said, "did you know that my ancestors came to America a hundred years before the American Revolution?"

It was information of which she reminded me often, always ignoring the fact that they were my ancestors as well as hers. "Yes, ma'am," I said.

Mother opened her mouth to say something, but settled with "Merry Christmas, Agnes," and took my hand and dragged me through the back door as if we were escaping a burning building.

Once outside, we trudged silently through the darkness across Grandma's yard toward our own. As soon as I felt we'd safely cleared earshot of the big house, I asked, "Where are we going to Mass tomorrow, Mama?" even though I knew the answer already.

"Camp Nine," she said, as if it should be a happy surprise.

I stopped in the snow. "Why?"

She walked around me and placed her hand on the latch of our gate. "It's close," she said, her voice rising and falling in a pleasant singsong manner that made her answer sound rehearsed. "They're our neighbors."

"Our neighbors?" My entire life, we'd had no real neighbors, other than Grandma and Grandpa, and although we barely interacted with them, they were family. The Japanese people couldn't be our neighbors. They were the enemy.

"It's not such a bad place," she said, the iron complaining as she pushed the gate open, "if you don't have to live there."

I shivered, refusing to move. "Mama, please. I don't want to go there."

We stood on opposite sides of the gate, our breath freezing in the night air. The electric light illuminating our backyard pierced through the bare branches, casting streaks of shadows across her face like camouflage stripes. "Chess," she said, evenly, "I didn't have any control over this situation with your grandfather. I wish those poor people had never come to Rook. But they're here. We're all standing around with our hands in our pockets like it's not happening. And that's wrong."

She parroted what I had heard Tom say: the Japanese were at Camp Nine for their own protection, not because they'd done anything wrong. But I was not to be dissuaded. The soldiers, the guns, and the barbed wire were not there just for show. And while I could abide it on the outside, I could not bring myself to go inside it.

"It's a prison," I said.

"The Delta is a prison," she said sharply, then caught herself. "We have a responsibility to make life a little better for each other," she said gently. "Now stop being such a silly goose. We'll go tomorrow and we'll have a wonderful time. It's in the Christmas spirit."

She let go of the heavy gate and it clanged closed behind us.

We walked slower than before. The sound of winter whistled through snow-tipped pine needles above our heads. Our footsteps crunched lightly and muffled in the stillness. "Now's a good time to tell you," she said, her words escaping as wisps that I could see.

Anxiety rushed over me. If there was something that she found difficult to tell me, it must be truly distressing.

"I've let the superintendent at Camp Nine know that, as soon as school starts in January, I'm available to teach art classes."

Her face was poised inquisitively, inviting my comment. How could I explain what I was feeling? We were all trying to pretend that Camp Nine was just a bad dream happening to other people, people we would never know. It didn't matter to me whether or not what had happened to the Japanese was right. It wasn't any of my business what a faceless government bureaucracy decided to do—as long as it didn't affect me. And yet, even at that age, I knew that was wrong, and some part of me resented her for making me face it.

She waited for my reaction. "Well?"

"I'm cold," I said, and raced up the steps into the warmth of our home.

———

As light broke on Christmas morning, my high-minded revelation had turned to selfish dread. It's hard now to remember it clearly. It only comes back to me in generalities, but I recall my apprehension fueled by the months of whispers and suggestions that had accompanied the arrival of Camp Nine and its ill-fated inhabitants. The omnipresent smoke curling from the distant smokestack conjured rumors of killings being carried out, with dangerous spies executed by gunfire and burned in the incinerator. The fact that no one ever heard shots ring out didn't seem to squelch the nightmarish tales. Camp Nine slept like a sedated-yet-dangerous beast across the tracks. No one but Mother seemed to have any desire to rouse it. The minutes slowed like hours as we neared the border, my unease looming until I could hear my own pulse clanging in my ears.

The ice had stopped falling, but there was no sun to be seen behind the thick clouds. Our Buick bumped over the railroad tracks and followed the still-slick road toward Camp Nine. But the sight that met me as we pulled to the entrance was amazing. I had expected a fortified stone prison, but instead, it resembled more a neatly arranged, if somewhat poorly constructed, village. The forest that had once covered the area was gone, and in its place were endless rows of buildings that seemed to be long, crudely crafted, storage sheds. But the smoke drifting from chimneys told me that there were people living in them, like an entire city of tenant houses.

Streets as wide as boulevards ran between the rows of houses, dropping off steeply into deep ditches on either side. We drove a short stretch to a parking lot where several mud-caked cars were parked, evenly spaced. An American flag hung limp and frozen on the flag pole. Mother shut off the engine and the car fell silent. She leaned over and patted my hand. "Come on."

We passed through a maze of buildings marked with the names Library, Gymnasium, and Camp Administration until we came to a common area where I caught my first glimpse of people.

If I find difficulty in remembering how different my expectations of the grounds were with reality, I can only relay that it was my encounter with the inhabitants that made me realize our community mistake. Certainly, the guard towers armed with marksmen and the miles of glinting barbed wire surrounding us clearly conveyed that this was a prison, but the people coming and going gave no hint that they would be considered prisoners. In contrast to the cartoon images in my head of depraved, bug-eyed fanatics, the people I saw looked not only normal but defiantly prosperous.

In their expensive coats and well-made overshoes, they didn't look like anyone I'd ever seen in Rook. A woman ahead of us wore a felt hat with a feather pinned to the side. Her husband, in a gray fedora and polished brown shoes, walked beside her, guiding her along the icy path with his hand on her elbow. Heading in our direction on a perpendicular sidewalk was a group of high school girls. They chattered excitedly, their straight hair swinging, their full skirts bobbing underneath their coats. We were all streaming toward the building named Community Center.

A man held the door open for us, and we entered the large, decorated room. Hundreds of people sat on long benches, men in suits, women in fur-trimmed dresses. At the front of the room was an impromptu altar fashioned from a folding table. There were no flowers, but it was festive with candles and wreaths of holly and berries. The only source of heat aside from the communicants, a puny space heater by the door, did little, if anything, to warm the freezing space inside the unpainted pine walls.

Mother motioned to a bench in the back, and we took our seats. In the rare times we'd been the lone whites in the company of groups of black families, I'd felt familiar and welcome, although in years since, I've wondered how welcome I'd really been. But, despite how ordinary these people seemed, in this place I felt entirely alien. Rook was my town, but this was a place apart.

People on all sides looked up from their missals and gaped. When Mother saw someone staring in our direction, she nodded and smiled broadly. Embarrassed, they pretended that they'd been looking at something else and had only accidentally caught sight of us. But, her friendliness infuriated me. In my discomfort at being an outsider, I had no desire to interact with anyone, and I wanted only for this ordeal to be over without drawing further attention to myself. In a stunning change of heart from only the half hour before, I was satisfied that no one here was suffering. I could leave these people with a clear conscience and I was ready to do so at the first opportunity.

Staccato footsteps echoed on the concrete floor and stopped. A woman stood patiently at the edge of our bench. Mother picked up her handbag and nudged me farther down the way.

As the lady took her place beside us, her family filed in, first her husband, then a younger man, a few years older than I was, caught somewhere between childhood and adulthood. I was riveted by the lady's pale skin and bright red lipstick. Her hair was drawn into a snood and topped with a stylish velvet hat, the verdant color of spring moss. She opened her missal and lowered her head toward the pages, praying the Hail Mary. It struck me as terribly odd that the image to which she bowed looked nothing like her—she was my Mary, blue-eyed and brown-haired, the exact picture in my own missal.

The father smelled faintly and pleasantly of aftershave, his graying hair combed neatly with grooming cream. Their son, his skin a rich, caramel color, leaned forward to brush snow from his gray trousers and his burnished shoes. His overcoat was tailored narrowly across the shoulders, in a design then in vogue. He peeled away his gloves, revealing fingers which were long and narrow, his nails trimmed and clean, the cuticles forming pale half-moons.

The door to the church opened and the processional began with three white-robed boys soberly marching the length of the room. The tallest of the three, a lanky boy of about my age, carried a crucifix thrust toward the ceiling. A smaller, younger boy cradled the oversized liturgical book in his slight arms, and the third awkwardly swung a bronze incense burner. Benches scraped against the concrete floor as the congregation stood. The priest concluded the procession, his big shoes kicking up the hem of his vestments. He made his way to the altar, then stopped and turned. Lifting his hands in the air, he intoned the greeting in a pinched voice that carried no regional distinction.

As the congregation bowed to receive his blessing, the door burst open and all heads swiveled at once to see a teenaged boy in unpressed trousers stumble inside. His shirttail hung loosely from the back of his coat. His collar stuck out unevenly. Annoyed, the priest paused, then continued despite the commotion as the boy slipped into our row and took his place with the family. I leaned forward, pretending to have dropped something on the floor, and stole a look at the father's face, which had grown hard. The mother's pale skin was flushed now with a crimson tinge.

The older, respectable brother suppressed a faint grin, but the younger one couldn't contain himself. A charming snort escaped from his lungs, and as he fought to regain his composure, a shock of shiny hair fell across his face. It was only then that I recognized him from the train. His was the face that had been peering at me the first day they had arrived in Rook.

He turned to catch me watching him. I jerked back, but it was too late. The last thing I saw as I sat upright was the most irresistible and mischievous grin I'd ever seen. Even in my baffled state, I couldn't help but smile in return.

Despite the strangeness of the surroundings and the absence of statues and other visual cues that I'd always associated with Catholic Mass, there were unique virtues to the service. There was no singing, and the priest from Los Angeles gave only the briefest of homilies. He talked of being strangers in a strange land and the Jews crossing the desert into Egypt. It was mercifully short, and, as the priest bade us in Latin to go in peace, I planned our discreet flight through a side door.

But escape was not to be. Mother was talking to the lady in our row.

"San Francisco," the lady said.

"Welcome," Mother was saying. "If there's anything I can do."

Her name was Sakura Matsui. Her husband was Hiroshi and their sons were Henry, the older, and David, the younger. Mr. Matsui, heavily accented, bowed when he spoke. Henry leaned forward to politely engage himself in the conversation, but David fidgeted and sighed, craning his neck around us as if he, too, were seeking relief from this insufferable gathering.

As the strained pleasantries died down, Mother lifted her coat from the bench, and Mr. Matsui glanced sternly at Henry, who sprang into action. "Allow me, Mrs. Morton," he said, rescuing the coat from her hands and draping it across her shoulders. She clutched the lapels, drawing them close to her neck, and murmured her appreciation.

The vast room was now nearly empty, the final stragglers just filing through the door. We took our place at the back of the line and made our way into the biting wind outside, while Mother chatted with Mrs. Matsui about her new job teaching at Camp Nine. I begrudged the excitement in her voice. I could now accept the presence of Camp Nine, but I did not want to be a part of it. It was all too strange and otherworldly. It might be true that the Japanese had to make the best of their sad and miserable reality, but I wanted nothing more than to retreat to the safety of the world I already knew—the one on the other side of the tracks.

As we walked away, David Matsui gazed at a lone hawk circling the leaden sky and shivered. Together we watched, and I expect we both envied it its freedom.

Chapter 5

As winter bore down on us until we could hardly stand another day of it, and finally turned toward spring, I became used to a new ritual, one I'd never before witnessed. Gradually, Mother had brought all of her bright dresses, once relegated to the back of her closet and shrouded in muslin sheaths, to the forefront, and each morning, after our breakfast, she cheerfully chose a different one to wear to work. Gone were the gray and black formless shifts to which I'd grown so accustomed. Her new look showed off her lovely shape, and she spent a great deal of time accessorizing with long forgotten trinkets and beads, arranging her hair, and applying delicate powder and lipstick in her favorite color, Shanghai Red.

Almost overnight, the focus of her attention had changed as well. She still asked me how I was getting on at school and ran her hands over my shoulders affectionately, but I was no longer the center of her world—she now had a real purpose of her own that had nothing to do with me.

One Saturday in early March, we enjoyed an early dinner of fried chicken and biscuits while Ruby Jean waited patiently for us to finish our meal. I don't know when the black people around us ate, for I never saw them put a bit of food to their lips. Even Ruby Jean, who had been a mother to my mother, who had nursed her in illness and taught her the gentle art of being a lady, never once ate a meal in our presence. I don't recall ever hearing her being instructed so—and that was the mystery of the relations between blacks and whites. The rules were so deep-rooted, the code of behavior was known to all.

Mother finished hurriedly, rapt as she had been all morning in piecing together a new Easter dress for me and anxious to resume her work. She thanked Ruby Jean for dinner and rose, but I took my time, savoring each morsel of crispy buttermilk batter and boorishly scraping my plate of the last bits of mashed potatoes. Mother joined Ruby Jean next to the sink and poured herself a glass of lemonade.

Ruby Jean's hands were soapy in the dishwater, and that alone would have caused the dropping and breaking of the dish. But she'd been preoccupied with something and it was time for it to come out.

Mother helped her pick the shards of china from the murky sink water, then said firmly, "Speak your mind, Ruby Jean."

"I might as well tell you, Miss Carrie. They's people up to no good."

I was unprepared for more upheaval. In retrospect, even though I hadn't the faintest idea how the black people in our community really lived, I had far more interaction with them on a daily basis than I did with the poor whites of the county. While I attended school with other white people and saw them walking the roads and working the fields alongside our black workers, I didn't know how they passed their days or what they thought of things. I naively assumed that my interests were their interests, and that our beliefs were their beliefs. While that was probably true in some form for most of them, it certainly didn't account for everyone. And there was a hidden radical element of which I was only remotely aware.

The original Ku Klux Klan, a backlash against Reconstruction, had flourished and died in other parts of the country, but had never reached into DeSoto County—there simply weren't enough people here after the Civil War for the carpetbaggers to want to bother with. DeSoto County's only community of the time, DeSoto City, a lawless pit of mud and incivility, was just a port for loading and unloading passengers who might disembark a paddlewheel arriving from Memphis or Cairo and take the train out of the Delta and into the hills beyond the Mississippi alluvial plain.

It wouldn't be until the turn of the century that DeSoto City grew into a proper river port with merchants, lawyers, banks, and an opera house. By then, the Klan had been reborn as a different organization entirely in the rise of the misguided patriotism that bloomed just as the twenties dawned. The Klan's goal was to restore Americanism to America and to banish all forms of inferior exoticism, racial or religious. Comprising the lowest form of white society, the new Klan represented the poor man's answer to all his problems. Its real aim was to ensure the survival, by any means possible, of his endangered niche in our world—one step above the black man.

Mother remembered it well. When she was a young girl, the new Klan was making its rise, handsomely paying organizers to recruit the disenchanted among the locals. Whether or not they believed in the ideology they preached, there was ten dollars to be made for each new recruit. The more frenzy they provoked, the more money organizers stood to gain. Night raids were conducted, not so much to enforce some vague code of honor, but to encourage enthusiasm for the group's ideas.

As immigrant Italians and Catholics, the March family had endured raids, threats, and fires. But Mother's personal problems with the Klan stopped when she became a Morton. Wealthy whites of good breeding were never members of the Klan, a fact little understood by outsiders. Underneath the obvious, the Klan's message of hate and intolerance was not a question of race. It was a message of economic opportunity. The Arkansas Delta aristocracy, as rough around the edges as it might be, had no need to oppress blacks through anonymous fear. The ruling class could simply expel a rebellious black man from his home, his family, and his chance to earn a living. Its opposition of the Klan was not so much that it felt a noble obligation to protect vulnerable blacks. The Klan threatened its valuable work force, the means through which its wealth was achieved.

I'd heard of marches in DeSoto City and even McHenry, but I'd never seen them. Mother had made sure I would not be exposed to that kind of senseless hatred. They paraded down the main streets of the towns around us every so often, hooded in secrecy, to remind all those they sought to control that they were there, then disappeared back into the woods. There were rumors of planned terror raids, but, as far as I knew, they were never conducted. And in Rook, the Mortons, who controlled all of the available employment opportunities, were Catholics. Anyone who would dare to openly belong to the Klan in our part of the county would have been foolish indeed.

But DeSoto City was a bit outside the Mortons' reach, and this was Ruby Jean's news: Mr. Ryfle had been gone for three days the week before, three days which had coincided with a break-in at the DeSoto City jail and the kidnapping and torture by an anonymous mob of a black prisoner accused of stealing bags at the train station.

Mother faced her squarely. "Are you sure, Ruby Jean?"

"Miss Carrie, you don't know the half of it," Ruby Jean said. "He been preaching over to the Kimble Baptist 'bout how this county done gone to the dogs. He got 'em all up in a tizzy over there." Ruby Jean had a source—her church sister, Mizelle Lewis, cooked for the pastor, Brother Akin.

"I'd heard they'd replaced Brother Akin," Mother said.

"It's worse than that. They got them a whole new church council. And Miss Carrie, I didn't want to tell you none, but I heard they got a beef about them Japanese folks."

Mother's voice rose. "Hammond Ryfle was paid to clear that land," she said. "I don't know how much, but it was a pretty penny, I can assure you." She clicked her tongue so loudly I could have sworn the sound bounced off the flowered wallpaper. "It's just like that old fool to take Walter's money and then complain about the result."

"Oh, Mr. Hammond, he smart," Ruby Jean said. "He know better than to go against Mr. Morton out loud. He say it ain't Mr. Walter's fault."

"Well, that's uncommonly thoughtful of him."

"No, ma'am. He say it your fault."

There was a loud bang as the base of Mother's glass hit the counter. "Oh, for heaven's sake! You're not serious, Ruby Jean."

"Yes, ma'am. That what I heard."

"Well, I'll have to have a word with Mr. Morton about that."

"Yessim, you might ought to."

Mother turned abruptly and retired to her sewing room.

My plate was empty, but my stomach felt nonetheless hollow. Ruby Jean was strangely quiet by the sink, and, as there was a sideboard between us, I couldn't see her face. Birds twittered peacefully outside the window, but the idea that there was subversion being plotted outside our house, as well, filled me with a sense of dread.

As I rounded the sideboard, she took my plate from me and placed it in the sink among the suds. I hung there alongside her, but she turned her back on me to signal that she no longer cared to discuss the matter. As she quietly washed and put away the rest of our dishes and retreated to the back porch to iron, I sat in the living room and flipped through the new *National Geographic* magazine. But the whole affair had driven me to such distraction, I was unable to even commit to it. Ruby Jean's news had me all unsettled and as frightened of an unseen enemy as I'd ever been of the Japanese. The Japanese were obvious by their appearance. But there was no way to tell who was the real enemy among us, and there were no armed guards and fences to protect us from them.

As the afternoon light filtered through the living room and streamed down the hallway, I wandered absently to my room and sat in my window seat. Across the yard, Ruby Jean traipsed through the forsythia hedge, basket in hand, undoubtedly carrying Willie Monroe's dinner. I bolted through the back door and ran to catch up to her, which wasn't difficult since years of hard labor had taken their toll.

"Lordy, girl," she said, "you ain't coming with me, is you?"

"You going to Willie's?"

"I am."

"Then, yessum," I said.

My plan clearly ran against her wishes. She paused along the path. "What for?"

"I like Uncle Willie. Please?"

"You got no business," she said brusquely, but turned on her heel and headed down the dusty road without further protest.

I strolled silently next to her, until we reached the road bridge over Black Bayou. Crooked and wild, the bayou cut a narrow swath through the county on its way to the river. Its impenetrable, chocolate-brown waters were home to countless turtles, lizards, and fish, including the fierce-looking remnant from prehistoric days, the alligator gar, with its bulging eyes and razor-sharp teeth. Dotted along the bayou's length was an occasional deep eddy, suitable for swimming only to the brave few. I was not counted among that number.

Not quite fifty yards upstream was the most notorious of all pools, one that was not entered by even the most intrepid. Nestled in a caved-in crook of the bayou was a deep pocket that had been carved from the bank by the swiftly moving current. The roots of giant cypress and oaks formed a living lattice as they reached from the bank to the base of the stream. The murky water inside the graceful, natural cage roiled with life. It was a water-moccasin den to end all others, and I never crossed the bridge without a fateful glance its way, wondering if they chose to live there because of the nearness to Cottonmouth Monroe.

Halfway across the bridge, Ruby Jean halted and closed her eyes. I stopped ahead of her and took a momentary glimpse at the snake pit, superstitiously believing I must pay some form of homage to it to safely pass. Beneath us, a stick spun round and round, encircled by dead leaves. Ruby Jean mumbled something low, then reached inside the pocket of her dress and pulled out a gray feather. Leaning over the bridge, she dropped the feather into the bayou, where it was caught up in the swirling water.

She leaned with closed eyes so precariously over the edge, I wondered if she might fall in. She growled deeply down in her throat and spit into the water after the feather. She made the sign of the cross, a motion she'd picked up from being in the March household but carried out without appreciation of its meaning, and resumed walking, more hastily, as if she couldn't get off the bridge fast enough.

Her actions needed no explanation. All of Ruby Jean's family believed strongly in ghosts, "haints" they called them. Her extended family, which included her uncle, Willie, and her cousins, Homer and Cecil, counted among their ancestors slaves who'd been converted to Christianity upon their arrival in America. They belonged to the AME, the African Methodist Episcopal Church, which was a most elegant and impressive name, and seemed in every way preferable to being a Catholic. I was fascinated by everything about Ruby Jean's church, right down to the colorful, cardboard fans featuring an advertisement by the black funeral home in McHenry. Mother had told me that they had their own bishop in Greenville, a black man who wore a purple shirt. Our own bishop from Little Rock was frightening, a severe, emaciated stick in a mitered hat whose long, yellow fingernails needed trimming.

But their forebears, and then they, had hung on to certain pagan practices, a form of voodoo, which they strictly observed. They managed to mesh these competing philosophies together seamlessly, hedging their spiritual bets, as it were. Ruby Jean often stopped during the day to mutter spells. If she dropped her broom, she walked in circles around it three times before picking it up again. Ruby Jean's voodoo was the one subject about which she would entertain no questions from me, but I was allowed to press the pocket of her apron to feel the tiny bone of a black cat which she carried for good luck.

We walked without speaking for a bit, but the lively fresh air of the afternoon seemed to have alleviated her mood. I decided to try my hand with her on the subject of the Klan. "Ruby Jean?"

"What now, girl?"

"Do you really think the Klan will march here?"

Our path veered away from the road and followed the edge of

the bayou. Up ahead, the row of drab tenant shacks hunkered against the black cypress tree line.

"I don't know, Chess. They'd be fools to."

"They can't hurt anyone at Camp Nine. There's too many soldiers there."

"Long's they stay on they side of that fence," she said, concluding the topic altogether. She brushed aside an overhanging muscadine vine and we continued on the path, which split down the middle, one part going to Willie's, and the other going on down to Homer's, Cecil's, and Ruby Jean's.

Like the others, Willie's shotgun house was arranged with one room after another, straight from the front door to the back. An African design that encouraged airflow through the structure, a shotgun house was so named because legend had it that a person could stand in the front door and shoot a shotgun, and the buckshot would go straight out the back door.

The houses that lined Black Bayou were gray, bare-wood cypress, their roofs fashioned of tin, and in the hot summertime, heat radiated in mirages disappearing into the sky. Each had a small porch running the length of the front. Willie's sported a broken-down divan with a crocheted blanket across the top and lace doilies on the arms.

When we arrived, Ruby Jean hoisted her basket against her hip and slammed her foot on the bottom step, pounding loudly. She hollered. "Willie!"

We listened, but there was no response. "The rascal might be asleep," she said. "I don't want to spook him." She stepped up to the top step and slammed her foot down twice. The decrepit porch shook. "Willie!"

"Hush up, woman," Willie called from inside. A cane scuffled against the floor and his withered brown hand appeared on the screen door handle. "I'm blind, sister. I ain't deaf." The screen door creaked open and he shuffled out onto the porch. He stopped and cocked his head. "Who's that you got?"

"Chess come with me," Ruby Jean said.

Willie's face cracked open into a wide smile and his milky eyes flickered in my direction. He trained them just to the side of me and grinned. "My, my. How you doin,' Little Miss?"

"I'm fine, Uncle Willie," I said. "Thank you."

Ruby Jean harrumphed to indicate she was there to accomplish something. "Sit yourself down, Willie. I brung you chicken and pie. Chess here done et all the biscuits."

Willie eased himself down with his cane and settled onto the divan. "Little Miss," he said again, as if he were weighing the sound on his tongue.

Ruby Jean set the basket next to him and pulled back the tea towel. "He'p yourself, Willie," she said, guiding his hand over the basket. "He'p yourself."

Willie pulled the meat from a drumstick and placed it in his toothless mouth. His head bobbed slowly as he chewed.

"I'm gone go make up your bed. You mind yourself around Chess," Ruby Jean said, disappearing into the house.

I didn't understand then what she meant, but it's clear to me now. Despite his simple appearance as a wizened and harmless old gentleman, Cottonmouth Monroe carried about him the air of a wizard. Ruby Jean guarded access to him and his secrets jealously, and his presence promised the temptation of seditious ideas. If there was a possible chink in the armor of our ordered society, surely it was Cottonmouth Monroe.

"How's your momma gettin' along?" Willie asked.

"She's fine, Uncle Willie."

"She still get them sick headaches?"

"Not so much any more," I said. It hadn't occurred to me to notice, but they'd come with less frequency since she'd begun at Camp Nine. Perhaps, I thought, Ruby Jean had been right. Mother had needed something more than just me to give her a sense of purpose. "Sometimes, though."

He nodded. "She always has been afflicted. Lord knows she got enough to set her off."

"I think Mr. Ryfle sets her off," I said. "And sometimes Grandpa does." I wanted to ask if he, too, knew of Mr. Ryfle's leanings, but I decided to let sleeping dogs lie. I'd been scolded more than once for repeating gossip I'd overheard in our house.

Willie sighed. "Any woman got to live in the middle of they two men liable to have to take to they bed now and again."

He shook his head and murmured low, as if grave thoughts had entered his mind. Ruby Jean was in the house. Surely no harm could come from my prying questions. "Uncle Willie," I said, "do you know what the bad blood is?"

His eyes turned toward the levee. "Yessum," he said.

"Ruby Jean won't tell me what it means."

His head began to move as regular as a heartbeat. A sound started deep down in his throat emerging as a low hum.

"Will you tell me?" I asked.

His humming gave way to a warbly singing. "You see its God's own will is what the Bible people say, strange things happening, happening in the land. Nations against nations rising up in this land. Kingdoms against kingdoms, you should understand." His foot thumped along to the rhythm of his bobbing head, but his singing was a half step behind and I found myself anticipating when each word would strike.

"Willie!" Ruby Jean crashed out of the house onto the porch. "I told you to behave yourself! Chess Morton don't need to be hearing no levee camp holler. You hush up."

His eyes pointed nowhere. "Yessum," he said, but his foot and his head kept on moving, as if the song went on in some place only he knew.

Ruby Jean stood between Willie and me, forming a wall between us. She lifted the basket from the bare boards of the porch. "Come on, girl," she said. "Let's get you on home."

The spring heat was green and heavy like a dream, and the grasshoppers began their shimmering racket. I followed Ruby Jean back down the path, turning long enough to see Willie before he faded from my sight. I waved to him, even though I knew he couldn't see it.

Chapter 6

Mother was a wildly popular teacher among her students at Camp Nine, and their parents and grandparents, beguiled by her charm and her desire to reconnect with her California past, clamored for classes of their own. Mother said the Japanese were naturally curious, and that learning new skills was an important part of their culture.

But she was getting as much as she was giving, and she eagerly took on Saturday classes for adults, allowing her even more time to spend at the camp. Although I had resisted accompanying her, once she began going on Saturdays, I lost my natural excuse. I didn't have school to hide behind, and she was so anxious that I experience what she considered a unique and historic opportunity to expand my horizons that I felt obligated to honor her enthusiasm.

She started my immersion slowly, at first bringing me along for the morning, where my duties included enduring the acrid smell of turpentine as I washed brushes out in the sink, and steadying the edges of large sheets of brown butcher paper while she halved them with sharp scissors. As weeks passed, we began staying after art class for lunch, and by April, I was spending entire days at Camp Nine. As I became accustomed to the place, it began to seem more real to me than the world outside. I was volunteering to go without Mother asking, and on Saturday mornings, I awoke actually looking forward to it because, like so many other things about which she was right, I found that, although it was tucked into the Delta, it was my chance to view the outside world, as surreal as the lens may have been.

The grounds of Camp Nine hummed with activity. Never willing to sit idly by, the Japanese taught classes in sewing and flower arranging, woodworking and metal shop, and, for some of the older people, the English language. The more I was there, the less apart I felt, and over time, I began to feel accepted. But I observed the unusual ways of the Japanese with wide-eyed wonder, for the education was also mine. I had never been exposed to adults who wanted to continue to learn things. Most of the adults in my orbit had never even finished high school.

Mother had a special fondness for the Matsuis. As a young bride newly arrived from Japan, Mrs. Matsui had lived only four blocks from Mother's old San Francisco neighborhood, though their districts were separated by custom. Although she was warm and friendly with Mother, Mrs. Matsui was shy with me and seemed unapproachable, so I kept a respectable distance and watched her refined manners without being obvious.

Mr. Matsui, usually stiff and formal, became loud and agitated when he spoke with Mother of his friend from San Francisco, a man named Korematsu, who'd been arrested for refusing to evacuate when ordered. He was imprisoned somewhere, and Mr. Matsui was hungry for information on what was happening to him. Sometimes, their conversations worked them both up into a froth, and their desire to challenge the status quo led to some fierce talk that worried me.

For two young men who could have been doing other things with their time, Henry and David tolerated my company admirably, and as the weather turned balmy, I spent many hours outdoors with them. Through our conversations, I learned their life histories, of Henry's plan to study engineering at the University of California, an offer rescinded because of the war and the relocation to Arkansas. I absorbed David's progress in the tenth grade and his accomplishments with the school's string ensemble.

Henry, the gentle overachiever, was his parents' favorite. He was quiet, studious and well-mannered, and as I thought of him often over the years, I came to realize that he represented their safe bridge to the new world. It took no more than a quick glance from Mr. Matsui to signal to Henry that some particular action was required to maintain the honor of the family.

Whether it was his status as the younger son, or just his natural personality, David did not measure up to Henry in those ways, and through his actions, he declared that he was not going to bother trying. Wild and unpredictable, David spoke loudly, often behaved inappropriately, and divided his time between playing the guitar and playing sports.

Henry was the reader in the family, his books stacked neatly on the makeshift bookcase he'd built himself. David's schoolbooks lay strewn about haphazardly, hidden under bedcovers, propping up his radio, or sitting, dust covered and dirty, under a tree while he tossed a baseball. Their spines were intact, as he hardly ever cracked them open.

Henry and I shared a love of history and literature, and as Mother had donated nearly our entire collection of books to the camp's library, we discussed the things we'd both read and loved. One evening, after supper, as Mother visited with Mr. and Mrs. Matsui inside their small apartment in the barracks, David lounged beneath a flowering arbor playing his guitar, while Henry and I compared our feelings about *Life on the Mississippi.*

I maintained that it seemed that Mark Twain couldn't have been talking about the same Delta that I knew, although he spoke with real affection for the long gone city of Napoleon, once located on the banks of the Mississippi River merely a mile or so from the Morton Plantation. A large river port, it had been an important stop during Civil War times, and ambitions for the town had loomed large. But the river had its own ideas, and Napoleon had slid from its banks and vanished beneath the waves shortly after, leaving nothing but occasional artifacts buried under towering vines.

It was such a romantic notion that it bore no resemblance to the dangerous, depressed region that I knew so well. But Henry countered that no one could really appreciate one's home except through the eyes of outsiders, and I've since come to accept that he was right.

David would have none of it. Sprawled on the ground, a guitar in his lap, and playing a lazy tune, he spoke his peace. "This place is a sinkhole," he said, to which I took umbrage and which illustrated, I would later realize, that stark criticism by a native is tolerated—from a stranger, it is not.

I bristled at his assessment of my home and told him as much. He looked up from his guitar, but his accomplished fingers kept pulling the strings. "Everybody around here plays like a rusty gate," he muttered.

Henry shrugged. "David had to leave all his musician friends in San Francisco. The high school band doesn't quite take their place."

In my desire to prove to David that we had merit, I spoke five words that would change the course of his life.

"You should meet Cottonmouth Monroe."

The suggestion was merely rhetorical, and I expect, if I hadn't used Uncle Willie's more colorful name, David might have just ignored my ill-placed comment. That David would ever cross paths with Willie didn't even seem possible. But Willie was the only example I could summon of anyone around who played an instrument. Even our little spinet piano, which Daddy had once played with some elementary skill, had sat silent for years, neither Mother nor I having any aptitude for it. Our only music came from the radio.

David's curiosity was piqued sufficiently to move him to stop playing. "Who's Cottonmouth Monroe?"

How could I describe Willie? He was only a blind man who lived on the bayou, and since I had never even heard him play, I was simply repeating a legend, which I realized with some measure of discomfort I had no business fostering.

"He plays the guitar," I said, hoping the conversation would go no further.

To my short-lived relief, David seemed satisfied with the answer.

He switched to a different tune, but his playing was unlike anything I'd ever heard before, the notes fat and full, played singly, not strummed in chords. He danced over the strings, the melody coming out fast in an odd, syncopated rhythm, demanding my attention.

"So," he said, stopping abruptly and grinning. "Where do I find this Cottonmouth Monroe?"

I believed, since Ruby Jean tried so hard to keep me from it, that Willie's gift must be a thing of awesome beauty. And I wanted so for David to think we were special. But I knew that Ruby Jean would have my hide if she learned that I'd given Willie away to a stranger, especially one whom the community feared. But that wasn't the only thing that stopped me. Although I wouldn't have been able to articulate it at the time, there was another problem, one much larger than the vague promise of Ruby Jean's wrath. It was possible for the white people of Rook to interact with the black people, and for the white people of Rook to interact with the Japanese. In each case, it was acceptable only if initiated by a white person. But contact between the blacks and the Japanese? How could I explain to David that it simply wasn't done? I didn't even understand it myself.

"I don't know," I said, trusting that, under the circumstances, a lie that prevented trouble was better than a truth that invited it.

David's interest in Willie seemed to go no further, and as evening wore on and we gathered for supper in the camp kitchen, I had forgotten completely about it. But I should have been suspicious when I noticed David in a brief, but lively conversation with Mother before we sat down. David was wild with his friends, but rarely engaging with adults, and I'd never before seen him talking so animatedly with Mother. As they parted company, he glanced my way with a sly grin, as though he were in a bit of trouble from which no harm would come.

We'd sat that evening at the table of Edo Hayashida, an ancient farmer from the California village of Castroville, and his company was so gentle and entertaining that I did not even notice that Mr. and Mrs. Matsui had disappeared from the group. It probably never would have occurred to me to think it unusual that they were not there, had it not been for Mrs. Matsui's sudden reappearance as Mother, Mr. Hayashida, and I left the camp kitchen just as darkness was falling. She hurried past, her head down and her face wrinkled with worry.

"Sakura?" Mother said as she passed. Mrs. Matsui didn't appear to have even heard. "What do you suppose, Edo?" Mother asked.

Mr. Hayashida adjusted his glasses. "Oh," he said, "everybody's kind of upset. Some men from the government were handing out forms, asking questions."

I noticed the normalcy of everyone else around us, in particular that no one else seemed visibly upset.

"Questions?" Mother asked.

He shrugged. "You know. More bureaucracy."

Mother's troubled gaze followed Mrs. Matsui through the crowd until she disappeared from sight.

It would be the first of many times I heard people talking in hushed tones about the mysterious questions, and in the succeeding months, those questions would change the face of the Matsui family in ways I wouldn't understand. But if Mr. Hayashida sensed their importance at the time, he didn't want us to know. He was eager to change the subject, and he leaned in close to Mother. "You being the art teacher, you'll want to see something."

An amused smile spread across Mother's face. "I'm intrigued."

"Come this way," he whispered, as if he had a secret treasure that he was hiding from everyone else. He turned down a sidewalk running between buildings, and we walked behind him and down the narrow confines of an alley.

In Mr. Hayashida's workshop, ten bare cypress knees rose from a rough bench. On a shelf under a window, odd shapes of polished and varnished wood told fanciful tales. Some were carved into birds, fish, and foxes. Others were simply fantastical, beautiful shapes.

"We call it *kobu*," Mr. Hayashida said, "the ancient art of Japan. We believe there is beauty in everything. You just have to be able to coax it out. This Arkansas cypress, it's A-number-1 for kobu. That bayou is full of it."

Mr. Hayashida ran his hand over a mountaintop with great care. "I had never seen anything like it before," he said. "In Japan, we had many beautiful trees. Not so much in California. These trees out here in the Delta, though, they really have a personality. Especially the cypress."

"Kobu," Mother said, tracing with her fingertip the head of a coiled snake.

"It's like this place has offered us a gift to say, 'Sorry you are imprisoned here,'" he said. "The place that you call, what, Black Bayou?"

"That's right," Mother said. She picked up a tiny, painted, wooden Baltimore oriole brooch and peered closely at it. "This is lovely."

Mr. Hayashida grinned shyly. "I have a million of those. Take it."

"Oh, no!" Mother said. "I couldn't."

Mr. Hayashida took her hand in his and pressed her fingers tighter around the carving. "Please," he said, "you'll hurt his little feelings if you don't take him home."

"Well," she said, relenting, "I couldn't let that happen."

"No, you couldn't let that happen." Tom Jefferies's voice, sounding from behind us, brightened the room. Mother whirled round to face him. "I heard you all were out here," he said, taking the bird from her hand and unhooking the safety pin on the back.

"When did you get here, Tom?" She closed her eyes as he leaned in close.

He slid his fingers underneath her collar and gathered the fabric together, carefully slipping the pin through her dress and hooking the loose end. "Just now."

He stood back and considered her. "Perfect. Edo," he said, "your best little bird yet."

Mr. Hayashida clasped his hands together and rocked back on his heels. "That's one lucky little bird."

Tom nodded. "Luckiest little bird in the world."

Mother, Tom, and I walked from Mr. Hayashida's shop through the darkness toward the Administration Building parking lot. Tom had been coming to Camp Nine off and on since Christmas, but since his visits were always during the week, I hadn't known about them. I suppose that Mother's insistence that I accompany her to Camp Nine was more than just her desire that I gain something of value from this new experience. She must have wanted me to know, eventually at least, about her relationship with Tom. In the weeks that followed, as his visits became more regular, I would find her searching my face for evidence of how I felt about him. She dropped gentle hints that it was so nice for her to have someone to talk to, someone who knew her in the old days.

But then it seemed that the entire convergence of circumstances was so providential as to be surreal. She not only had Tom back. She now had an entire community of people who, although they were in many ways vastly different than she, had some shared experiences with her other life in California.

She needn't have worried about my accepting Tom. In my own way, I was as hungry to have a man inhabit our lives as she was. And in that time of war, there was no more comforting and exhilarating presence than a high-ranking officer. I welcomed his company with joy. There was so much unspoken between them, and much more still unspoken between Mother and me, I wanted to know the story. And there were times I found myself moments from asking, but I kept quiet. It was a kind of superstition I had, that if I asked for too much information, the spell would be broken. She would wake up, Tom would be gone, and we would be alone again.

Across the quiet camp grounds, the Administration Building was closed for the evening and dimly lit from within by a scattering of metal desk lamps. Mother was the only staff person who didn't live on the grounds of Camp Nine. The dozens of teachers, administrators, secretaries, and maintenance personnel that had been recruited from distant cities occupied small cabins along the eastern edge of the camp. They had no transportation, but there was nothing interesting enough to do and nowhere appealing enough to go beyond the borders of the camp that warranted travel out. At the end of the day, the workers simply moved to another side of the vast complex, leaving the buildings dark.

The soldiers who patrolled the grounds lived in pockets of barracks that ringed the boundary of the camp. There were several contingencies on duty at all times, but they always seemed to be somewhere in the distance, up in the towers, or walking the fence lines. They were merely specters in the shadows, faceless shapes behind windows, floating dots on the horizon. Only when Tom was with us would we ever have any interaction with them, and then it was steeped in formality.

Across the field, a porch light flickered on a house I'd known to be unoccupied for years. I would soon spend many days there as it became sparsely trimmed with a few pieces of furniture, curtains, and cushions sewn by Mother, and a German shepherd named Gretchen borrowed from Camp Nine for my amusement. It would be where Tom Jefferies conducted his private, double life.

The thing I remember most vividly about Mother's classroom was the light. Like all camp buildings, the room was basic and spare. Horizontal rows of unfinished pine made up the floor, and vertical lines of pine intersected them, running up the walls. Across the ceiling, bare beams of the same rough wood, riddled with knotholes, comprised the joists and exposed the electrical wire and bald light bulbs. But Mother refused curtains and the light flooded in the windows, glowing in the morning, glaring at midday, and fading to sad, waning shadows in the evening. Students sat at long tables, while Mother paced the floor among them, offering gentle advice and warm praise. If they were deep in occupation of their work, she sometimes stood by the open window, staring across the fields beyond the camp toward the bayou, her thoughts kept firmly to herself.

Finished work was tacked onto the walls or hung from clips on one of several clotheslines that traversed the room. Mr. Hayashida had presented Mother with the gift of a dozen or so easels he'd made, and she'd arranged them haphazardly about the room, rotating the work of each student, never promoting an accomplished one over a struggling one.

One Saturday morning, Mother, surrounded by a gaggle of ladies alternating between English and Japanese, leaned over a wooden table with a snub-nosed pencil in her hand and drew on a sheet of paper stretched across the plywood top. "My heavens, I loved the Kabuki theater," she said brightly to the group. "As best as I can remember, this is what they were wearing. Does this look right?"

But no one responded. They'd enlarged their circle and occupied their eyes looking elsewhere. Mrs. Matsui was standing quietly to the side, clutching a bundle of white fabric.

Mother laid down her pencil. "Good morning, Sakura."

"Ah," Mrs. Matsui said, softly. "Carrie." She nervously folded and unfolded the fabric in her hand.

"We're planning the designs for the theater paintings," Mother said.

The other women shrank back and broadened their circle to let Mrs. Matsui pass. She came forward and politely inspected the sketches. "Yes," she said. She laid the fabric on the table and took several tiny steps backward, a silky French twist gleaming atop her head. "I ask you to honor my family, to paint for me a tiger on my son's *senninbari*."

The other women exchanged uncomfortable glances.

Mother unfolded the loose jacket of hand-stitched panels. Except for a large empty area on the back, it was dotted overall with red pencil marks that formed a grid.

Mother turned the senninbari over in her hands, then sat down. "A tiger?"

Mrs. Matsui remained standing, her head bowed. "Yes."

Mother opened her mouth to speak, but nothing came out.

Mrs. Matsui bowed so that her carefully arranged hair was plainly visible. "Carrie. Please."

Rolling up her sleeves, Mother pushed her drawings to the side as the other women crowded around the table. She picked up a pencil and began sketching on the fabric, her hands flying lightly over the table, until the basic outline of a tiger emerged.

Mrs. Matsui watched for a while, then wandered to the edge of the room. The scattered shouts of a group of boys playing football on the field outside filtered in through the glass.

"This is very unusual, Sakura," Mother said, pausing to get her perspective straight. "Is this a theatre costume?"

A coach's whistle blew.

A murmur rose from the other women, but Mrs. Matsui peered absently out the window. "No," she said. "It is for Henry."

Mrs. Yoshioka leaned in close to Mother. "*Senninbari* means 'thousand-person stitches,'" she whispered. "The tiger is courageous. He can wander far from home and return safely. All senninbari have the tiger. For good luck to come home to mother and father. From the war."

Leather helmets crunched.

Mother nodded. She narrowed the eyes of the tiger. His lean body curved inward, ready to strike his prey. She opened her paint box and pulled a brush from the water. Broad, bright strokes of red and orange filled in the stripes. "When are they leaving?" she asked softly.

Mrs. Matsui's back was straight and still. Someone coughed.

"One month," said Mrs. Ochi. "Only one month to get one thousand stitches in the senninbari."

Mrs. Matsui turned, her shoulders back and her face held high. "Plenty of time. I have a thousand friends to make the stitches."

And, with that, I learned that my friend, Henry Matsui, was leaving us. I couldn't have known then what it would mean to me, or that Mrs. Matsui's thousand friends would disappear from her life. So many things lay ahead, but it would only be in looking back that I would see them all connected.

Chapter 7

Although it's since declined like so many Delta towns, in those days, McHenry was a bustling railroad hub. Its long streets, laid out neatly beneath oaks and poplars, ran lengthwise north to south along the major highway between Little Rock and Louisiana. Since it was not a county seat, it lacked a courthouse, but prosperous grocers, druggists, dry goods stores, a bakery, and even a jewelry shop lined the business district, and an imposing hotel enjoyed a healthy trade next to the railroad depot.

On Saturday night, after I'd taken in a double feature at the Ritz Theatre so that Mother could do her shopping in peace, she was waiting for me in front of the HobNob Café.

The HobNob, which occupied a separate space in the center of town, was typical of most small-town lunchrooms of the time. Although the majority of the local population was black, the café was whites only. Black patrons could approach the back door and order something to go on a cash basis, but they were forbidden access by the front door. A smoky private room in the back of the café hosted the Lion's Club on Tuesdays, the Rotary Club on Wednesdays, and the Chamber of Commerce the first of each month, all of them groups of white men who controlled the local businesses and who fancied themselves philanthropists of one sort or another.

Stiff, uncomfortable wooden chairs and red-and-white checkered tablecloths crisscrossed the main dining room. The tables, topped with baskets of crackers and bottles of peppers floating in vinegar, were arranged four across and the back wall was lined with mirrors. The owner, Irene Polanski, buzzed through the room at mealtimes in her stained apron, taking orders, chatting up patrons, and calling everyone "sweetie."

When we entered, the cafe was swarming with well-to-do patrons.

"Sit yourself!" Irene called over her shoulder as we stepped inside the glass door. A waitress stood at the cash register punching buttons, a pencil stuck behind her ear. A bubble gum machine perched on a cylindrical metal stand next to a rack of newspapers for sale. A man and woman brushed past us on their way to the exit, stopping at a vending machine to buy a pack of cigarettes.

I started across the room toward a free table against the mirrored wall. Mother navigated an armload of powder-blue boxes from Feibelman's Department Store until we reached our destination, and she set them on the floor, tucked them up under the table, and chose the chair against the wall. I took a seat across from her, my back to the other diners, and watched the busy street scene reflected in the mirror.

Irene was right behind us, balancing a tray with two dripping water glasses, menus tucked underneath her wrinkled arm. She plunked down the glasses, tossed aside the tray, and stole a chair from the next table. "Put your things up here, Carrie," she said, dragging the chair leg with her foot. "Lord knows there's all kinds of grease on that floor. We been so busy, I ain't had no time to even sweep up yet."

Mother scooted back her chair and bent, lifting the boxes one at a time and stacking them in the free chair.

Irene waved the cardboard menus at us. "Y'all don't need these, do you, sweetie?"

Mother placed the last, small box on top. "You know what I want. Chess?"

"Yes, ma'am. The usual." I felt impossibly sophisticated to have a "usual."

Irene scribbled our orders without further conversation, then efficiently retreated to the kitchen, and returned moments later with a glass of iced tea, a sweating Coke bottle, and our sandwiches. She pointed the sharp pencil lead at Mother's stack of boxes. "What pretties did you get?"

"Feibelman's was having a sale," Mother said sheepishly, uncomfortable with having spent more on clothes that afternoon than Irene would make in a week. "But there were a couple of things I needed."

The kitchen bells dinged. Irene turned to another waitress. "Get that burger and chicken salad for me, will ya, Frankie?" She planted herself at our table, and I wondered if she might pull up another chair and sit down. "Let me see what you got, Carrie."

I was at a loss to explain Mother's desire for a store-bought dress, as accomplished as she was as a seamstress, and I was as anxious to see what she had purchased as was Irene. As Mother retrieved the largest box from the bottom, untied the ribbon, and lifted off the top, the reflection of Audrey Ryfle, Mr. Ryfle's daughter and Jesse's big sister, sitting at a table by the front door with two other levee girls caught my eye.

I had not seen Audrey in a couple of years, since she'd completed eighth grade, the highest grade attainable at the Kimble School. Since then, she'd blossomed into an even lovelier young woman, and despite the shabbiness of her clothes, she was radiantly beautiful in a fresh, wholesome way.

The other girls leaned across the table toward each other and chattered away, but Audrey was paying them no attention. Her eyes were glued to Mother, who was pulling back the tissue paper inside the box, revealing a breathtaking dress of white-and-yellow-striped silk. Around the waist was a grosgrain ribbon belt.

"My stars," Irene said, "if that don't beat all. If only you had somewhere around here to wear it."

"Oh," Mother said, "you never know."

"When you decide, you let me know," Irene said with a lascivious wink. "I just want to walk behind you picking up the crumbs." She slapped a thin, white ticket on the table and dashed off as the edges of the white paper soaked up a ring of spilled iced tea.

As the ink began to bleed, Audrey's voice startled me. I hadn't noticed her approach.

"Miss Morton?" she said. "I'm sorry to interrupt your supper."

Mother rescued the paper ticket from its bath and dabbed it with a napkin. "That's quite alright, Audrey. How are you?"

"Fine, thank you."

"And your parents are well?"

"Yes, ma'am."

"What are you doing with yourself this summer?"

"Well," Audrey said, "that's what I come to talk to you about. See, I had a job in the office over to the seed store in Kimble, but that's all played out now that there ain't no more planting." She flinched, as if she'd just spilled a secret. "I mean, *isn't* any more planting. I was wondering if you thought I might get on over to Camp Nine."

Mother searched her face. "How would your parents feel about that?"

Audrey shifted uncomfortably. "I expect they'd say okay, long as I'm bringing in some money."

Mother lifted her glass and took a sip. "I'm not so sure about that. Your mother and father feel—well, let's just say they feel rather strongly against the Japanese."

"Yes, ma'am, I know. But they also feel real strongly about me bringing home money. I don't know that they need to know where I get it."

Mother glanced up sharply. "How old are you now?"

Audrey bit her lip. "Sixteen." She paused. "Next month," she added meekly.

Mother picked up her sandwich. "If you'll come round the house Monday afternoon, I'll see what I can do. Alright?"

Audrey's face broke open in relief. "Thank you, Miss Morton. Thank you so much."

"But, Audrey."

"Yes, ma'am?"

"You will have to have your parents' permission. Understood?"

Audrey hesitated, then nodded firmly. "Yes, ma'am. Thank you." She disappeared through the glass door. From the window, I saw her long braid emerge onto the lamp-lit city street, then blend into the crowd and vanish.

I waited a moment as the question framed itself in my head. "Did you talk to Grandpa about Mr. Ryfle and the . . ."

Mother raised her finger before I'd finished. "Not out loud, honey." She looked about to see who might be listening. "He thinks it's just idle talk," she said softly. "But I don't believe that. Hammond Ryfle has circulated a petition around the Baptist church trying to get Camp Nine closed. Not that he stands a chance. But if Audrey goes to work there, maybe it will shut her father up once and for all."

If only it had been that simple.

Even now, I can't be sure how old Ruby Jean was then. Of course, anyone over the age of forty was positively antique to me, but I'm sure that the hard life she'd endured had aged her before her time. Mother said that, in the old days, Ruby Jean put in a full day's work, from before sunup to beyond suppertime with the Mortons, and then walked the long distance to the March household to do it all over again from evening well into the night. To compound things, in the summers, she often spent days working in the fields chopping cotton to help her cousins make the meager sharecrop they farmed in addition to their regular laborers' duties to the Mortons. As a result, by the time I knew her, she suffered severe bouts of arthritis.

One day, after a night's violent thunderstorm had stricken and then passed, she had made it to our house in the morning, but by dinnertime, she could hardly move about the kitchen. She'd sliced some tomatoes and gotten some grits going, but when she tried to knead her yeast rolls, it was clear that she was in deep pain.

"Ruby Jean, look at us," Mother said. "Walt's not here anymore, and I know Chess and I don't need you to make us dinner. If you don't sit down for a few minutes, I'm going to drive you home. Now sit!"

Ruby Jean eased herself into a chair, but we probably both knew that Mother's threats were hollow. Ruby Jean wouldn't take her pay if she hadn't put in a full day's work.

"I can't sit, Miss Carrie," Ruby Jean said. "I gots to take Willie his dinner. He won't eat if I don't bring him something."

"I'll go!" I said.

Mother eyed me strangely, but Ruby Jean was outright indignant. "No, ma'am," she said, pulling herself upright, and shaking her head. "Uh, uh."

Mother sighed. "Now, what could it hurt?"

"It could hurt plenty," Ruby Jean said, struggling toward the refrigerator. "Chess got no business running loose down to the bayou." She opened the refrigerator and pulled a cold plate of ham from the shelf.

Mother smiled. "Chess isn't a little girl anymore, Ruby Jean. You and I have got to get used to that fact."

It wasn't just Ruby Jean's desire to shield Willie from my intrusive questions that fueled her refusal. A white child would not have walked alone through the black community. Every town in the Delta, even a tiny burg like Rook, had both white and black sections, with the black inhabitants vastly outnumbering the white ones. Larger, louder, and more colorful, the black sections were separated by a thick rope of custom.

But there were written rules as well. I recall once, on a trip to Pine Bluff as a small girl, having to go to the bathroom, badly, and being in such a clamor when we finally stopped at the filling station that I raced to the first door I saw. When I emerged, Mother waited placidly, but a small, disgruntled crowd of men had appeared, watching me as the door opened. Above the door was a sign: "colored." I had breached the decorum. I can only imagine what would have happened if the circumstances had been reversed, if I had been a hurried black girl in search of a bathroom and had rushed into the door marked "white."

Ruby Jean winced in pain and relinquished the plate to the counter. She rubbed her back and sighed. "Go ahead on, then," she said reluctantly. "But you tell Willie I said to mind his manners."

Although the sun shone brightly as I carried a full basket in both hands down the gravel lane, I approached the Black Bayou bridge with not only respect toward the bayou and its serpents. I felt a new trepidation at both being out alone and visiting the secretive Cottonmouth Monroe without Ruby Jean's interference. The rain-swollen bayou swirled at a fierce pace underneath the bridge, tearing at the low-hanging branches and pushing walls of debris as it thundered past. I gave deference to the snake pit upstream, but the high, rapid water had covered up any evidence of it.

Thick mud flew from my boots as I rapped them sharply on the bottom step, in imitation of Ruby Jean. "Uncle Willie? Uncle Willie!"

There was a scooting of chair legs and a shuffle of leather heels. Willie's gray head materialized, filtered in the dark space behind the torn screen. "Little Miss?"

"It's me, Uncle Willie. Ruby Jean's arthritis has got her down today."

His broad smile shone through the brown mesh. "Well, well. Come on in. Come on in."

As the screen door creaked on its hinges, I climbed the steps and wrenched off my boots. Willie held the door for me and waited until he heard me pad past him in my stocking feet, then he let it shut gently behind me. "Sit down, Little Miss."

We took our places opposite each other, Willie on a weathered couch, and I in an upholstered chair that had seen its better days decades before. I set the basket on the low table between us. Willie pawed through it until he landed on a sandwich. "Ruby's down in her back?" he asked, disappointed that he'd not been brought a hot lunch.

"Yessir."

There was a stillness in the air that made it seem as though time itself had stopped moving. It was my first time to be inside the home of Willie Monroe and my eyes took in every image: the flowered wallpaper, the potbellied stove, the threadbare furniture covered with quilts I recognized to have been made by Ruby Jean. On the wall, right next to a picture of FDR straight out of *Life* magazine, a blond Jesus pulled open his gown to expose his bleeding heart. Underneath the pictures, an assortment of torn wallpapers, all patched together to cover the bare cypress walls, were peeling and falling away like the fragile bark of a sycamore tree.

Willie unwrapped the waxed paper and gnawed at the edge of the bread. "Virginia ham and honey," he said, chewing. "She's a good woman, take care of an ole coot like me."

In the corner of the room, an odd contraption leaned against the wall. It was a board with a nail in each end, a single wire strung between them. "Is that a guitar?" I asked, realizing as soon as I'd said it that Willie couldn't see what I was talking about.

He stopped in the middle of his sandwich. "Which one, Little Miss?"

I hesitated, not knowing what to call it. "It's only got one string."

Willie resumed his dinner. "You talkin' 'bout that jitterbug?" he said between bites. "Go ahead on and pick it up, then. Don't be afraid."

I took the few steps required to cross the tiny room and lifted the crude wooden instrument in both hands, inspecting it closely.

"It's called a jitterbug? Like the dance?"

"Yessum, that's what they call it. But they wasn't named after no dance. Was the other way around. I been making jitterbugs since

I was a little one. I made that one there for that boy from California. He say he didn't want to tote it on home. I told him leave it be. He come over every now and again and play on it."

"What boy?" I asked.

His dead gray eyes sparkled, pleased that he had a secret on me. He grinned at nothing in particular. "You know that boy. Say you tol' him 'bout me."

"David Matsui?"

He nodded. "That the one."

We could all see that David and his family were different. In a place where there was not, and never had been, anyone of Asian descent, one look at their faces set them immediately apart. But I realized that to Willie, David was just that boy from California. He surely knew why David was here. He must have known that it had to do with David's being Japanese. But it told me something about all of us, that we categorize each other according to our similarities and differences. Willie couldn't see David. But he could hear him. And his ears told him that David wasn't from around here.

Willie stared away, past me. "I be out on my porch, picking a tune, and he stop by. Say he like my sound. We pick a bit. Want me to teach him my tunes. Boy's a quick study. I bet he know fifteen or twenty songs by now."

He reached for the jitterbug and I placed it in his grasp. "That little boy sure like the Delta music. Ask me to show him how to play this thing."

How David had escaped from Camp Nine without detection, I didn't then know. But in my mind, I imagined his carefree, easy gait ambling along the gravel road with the levee looming in the distance, the crickets whirring during the middle of the day. He must have felt as though he'd been swept up by a storm and thrown into the Land of Oz.

Willie took the jitterbug, walked to the far end of the room, and placed the blunt end against the wall. The way he explained, since the instrument had no sound box, the most common practice was to nail it to the side of the house. When played, the entire house became a giant instrument.

To demonstrate the technique, Willie pressed the jitterbug flush against the wall. He plucked the lone string, and the scuffed wooden rail clucked like a chicken. Then he ran his bony finger down its length and an eerie, high-pitched scream rumbled through the walls. In the course of less than a minute, it sounded as though ten different things lived between the thin walls.

"Boy like the levee-camp hollers most of all," Willie said. "He can't get enough of them."

"Why doesn't Ruby Jean want me to hear the levee-camp holler?" I asked.

Willie's lean, hollow-cheeked head swayed back and forth. "Ruby funny that way," he said finally. "The holler make her think of bad times."

"Were you in the levee camp, Uncle Willie?"

"Yes ma'am, was in the levee camp ten years. Drove a hook team. Get up three thirty every morning building that ole levee right out there. Go harness you up some mules, then go git your breakfast, and by the time you get on out to the grass, it be light enough to work. Them ole mules'll kill your soul with they back feet, you don't treat 'em right."

His filmy eyes sparkled with the visions only he could see. "You could hear the mule skinners up and down that levee before sunrise to pass sundown. I could tell a man a mile away by his holler."

"What was yours?"

"Go on out to the porch, Little Miss, and grab ole Willie's gitbox. Ruby ain't here to fuss none. Ever'body got to hear the holler once in they life."

FDR grinned at me as I tore through the screen door and grabbed Willie's sun-warmed guitar from against the porch post, remembering Ruby Jean's admonishments, but choosing to ignore them. I carried the guitar inside, and he took it from me carefully, as if it were a favored child. The rickety divan creaked as he leaned forward and strummed a couple of chords. He twisted the knobs on the ends until he was satisfied that it was in tune, then bent deeply over the guitar. He hung his head low, thumping the box and bobbing his neck in time.

His eyes closed, he pinched the frets tightly, and the strings began to weep in high, sad tones. He raised his face and opened only one side of his mouth to sing along. The words emanated from his entire body in the form of a whole, round hum. "Pestilence and hurricanes and they also talking war. You see its God's own will is what the Bible people say, strange things happening, happening in the land. Nations against nations rising up in this land. Kingdoms against kingdoms, you should understand."

He slowed his strumming and thumped his thumbs against the wooden sound box. His edgy voice sounded like that of a ghost. "If I feel tomorrow, like I feel today, if I feel tomorrow, like I feel today, stand right there and look a thousand miles away."

His voice quavered and warbled, then dropped down to a low moan. "This here what they call the blues, Little Miss. You get the blues when life get you down, and you can't do nothing but sing it out loud. Back in the levee camp, you ain't got nobody. You all by your lonesome self. Colored folks can't tell nobody the truth 'bout the things that happen to them. So they bury it in song. Blues song don't never mean what it say. You got to listen past the words to find the truth."

He cried the loneliest sound I'd ever heard, a wail of despair that brought up the hairs on my arms and sent a shiver through my body.

He stopped and pointed his face at me. "You ask me one time, Little Miss, what was the bad blood. There 'tis, Little Miss. There 'tis."

I wanted to run, not from Willie, but from the pain that was balled up in his gaunt, shriveled body. But I was glued to the spot by the suspense of the story he wasn't telling me.

He resumed a gentle strumming, a bit lighter now. "That boy, David, he know the blues. Say it speak to him like no other. He lonely, too. Away from home. Got no one to show him the way."

"I'm sorry, Uncle Willie."

His face, leathered and angular as a turtle, turned slowly toward me. His brows knitted. "Now what on earth you got to be sorry for, Little Miss?"

"I didn't know David would come find you. I was just talking."

He relaxed into a soft grin. "Oh, you never know. Some things just meant to be, young lady. The Lord, He work in mysterious ways."

His fingers ran the length of the guitar neck and cried out a moan, then brought down a tender melody that spoke straight to my heart. Willie shook his head. "His will be done," he said.

Chapter 8

It was only recently that I saw the photographs of the suicide tucked away in Mother's cardboard box of memories.

Leo Togashi was one of Henry's friends. Strong and sinewy, he had been the anchor of the men's freestyle swim team at the University of Southern California. Relocation to Arkansas had cut short his future, and his teammates went on to find great athletic acclaim without him. The shame of his imprisonment and the rage of his helplessness to do anything about it sent young Leo to the railroad tracks, where he lay across until the late night train from McHenry flew over him without even stopping.

In the pictures, from some angles, he appeared to be resting, maybe sleeping off a hard drunk along the tracks, his khaki clothes rumpled but otherwise undisturbed in the gravel, his arms hanging loosely by his side.

But the next view showed only his head, face down, between the ties. A solid steel rail separated the two parts of him.

The day after Leo's death, the students in the Saturday class for ladies sat in a circle, whispering. The atmosphere was strange and tense, and while ordinarily I would have happily done nothing but watch them paint and observe the tangled mass of brilliant blue morning glories covering the arbor outside the window, that day I felt the need to prove myself useful. But there were only so many brushes to wash, and precious little else to do. I waited for Mother to approach the sink, then asked her what all the discussions meant.

When she told me the news of Leo, I was aghast. I'd seen him only a few days before, and like almost all of the Japanese in camp, he'd betrayed no sign of his troubles. He'd smiled and joked with other boys while I waited nearby, envious of what appeared to be their carefree friendships.

"What happened?"

She took her time studying a variety of boar-bristle brushes in the can where she kept the dry ones. "He killed himself, honey" she said.

She knew "why" was my next question, so she turned to face me to save me from asking. "He left a note. He just couldn't take it any more."

I glanced furtively at the ladies in the corner, who were muttering fiercely. "But it doesn't seem so bad here. Everybody seems to like it."

"It's hard to explain, Chess. Some of the children are happy, I admit. But what's happened here shouldn't happen to anybody. Some of them are so ashamed to be here, they just can't accept it. Some of the men committed suicide back in California to keep from having to come at all."

What was my mother thinking during that conversation? She'd tried so hard to both protect me from the harsh realities of life, and yet at the same time, come to appreciate the hardships of others. Here she was, keeping her voice low, explaining to me in the most matter-of-fact tones that there were people around us who had lost all hope, who saw no other way to cope with their loss than to end it altogether. Did she know then, as I would some day come to know, that the Japanese were so strong, and yet so fragile—that their strength and stoicism could also be their undoing? Rather than rail against the system that would condemn them this way, some of them would choose to keep their despair inside until it destroyed them. Even among themselves there was disagreement. Mother had told me that Mr. Matsui's hero, Mr. Korematsu, was reviled by even his family for defying the evacuation.

In the corner of the room, the ladies' voices swarmed like a hive of bees. I tried to eavesdrop on what was being said, but there was too much Japanese sprinkled in with the English for me to follow the conversation.

Leo's suicide, while immensely sad, was not the subject of the dialogue, Mother told me. There was another, more pressing problem. Leo Togashi was a Shintoist.

The exotic religions of Catholicism and Buddhism were surprisingly free to be practiced at Camp Nine. As I learned that first Christmas Day, the Maryknollers, who had served the Los Angeles Japanese community for years, posted a priest for the small number of Catholics, which included the Matsuis. Buddhism, on the other hand, posed a special logistical problem. At the outbreak of the war, many of the Buddhist priests were arrested, along with other community leaders, and imprisoned in special camps in the West. But as they were released to join their families in the general camps, they organized churches and youth leagues.

But Shinto was different. The ancient religion of Japan, it was Shinto that conferred on the emperor his supreme power and it was the country's state religion. Although many of Camp Nine's inhabitants were loyal Shintoists, the practice of their religion was officially banned. Many Shintoists blended their beliefs and rituals seamlessly with the Buddhists, and others took their beliefs underground. But the Shintoists were strict in their funeral practices. Leo would have to be cremated. And then his ashes would have to be buried.

And the Kimble Baptist Church was the only white cemetery—even a moderate like Brother Akin couldn't push through approval for a Japanese funeral.

I didn't know then what Mother was thinking, but she assumed that preoccupied air I knew so well that predicted that she was going to shake things up.

As was customary of grand, old houses of the South, Grandma's had a separate cookhouse to protect it from the heat and fire generated from cooking on woodstoves. Even though it had been electrified years before I was born and by then sported a modern indoor kitchen, some traditions died hard, and Odessa still cooked all of Grandpa and Grandma's meals in the small wooden building steps from the big house.

Behind the cookhouse was a porch that once had been whitewashed, but it had not been properly cared for over the years as Odessa's age advanced and her health declined. There remained patches of white paint on the rough wooden posts holding up the low roof, but most of the cypress with which it had been built was bare, exposing it to destructive elements and hungry insects. It was on the porch that Odessa tended to Grandma's linens, Parisian by way of New Orleans, with a wringer washer, and tacked them onto a clothesline, their dainty, intricate lace hems inches from the bare dirt ground. A few steps away, she unloaded their trash onto a big heap to wait to be carried off and burned by Cecil.

Just off to the side of the porch grew a giant mulberry tree. Although anything having to do with Grandma and Grandpa worried me silly, I often snuck into their yard just to climb the mulberry. Tall and stately, its lower branches were low and evenly spaced, which made it ideal for climbing to the top to retrieve the ripe, purple mulberries that appeared in the summer.

I was halfway up the tree when a car engine rumbled up the dirt road that wound behind the big house, loud enough to be Grandpa's Lincoln. I wrapped my hands around the trunk and crouched in the upper branches where I couldn't be seen.

The engine died, and a car door slammed.

"Odessa?"

It was Grandpa.

"Odessa?"

The screen door to the cookhouse creaked open and Odessa emerged.

"Yessir, Mr. Walter?"

"Where's Cecil?"

"I don't know, Mr. Walter. He ain't here. Ain't been here since I give him his breakfast this morning. What's the matter, sir?"

"Buck's down."

Buck was my daddy's horse, a magnificent buckskin, seventeen hands high, the color of honey with an ebony mane. Since Daddy's death, he'd been kept out on the place and I saw him only in my memory.

"Oh, Lord, Mr. Walter. Say that ain't so."

"I need Cecil to shoot him."

"Maybe he up to the thousand acres."

"May be. If you see him, tell him I need him."

"Yessir. I'll tell him."

Grandpa's boots crunched on the pebbles of the walkway as he made his way to the house. I waited until the door had slammed and the latch had clicked closed, then I clambered to the lower branches and jumped to the ground, just as Odessa passed, carrying a basket of wash toward the clothesline.

She leapt from the walkway when she saw me. "Chess Morton! You scared me half to death. What you be hiding for?"

"I wasn't hiding. You just couldn't see me up in that tree."

"I couldn't, for a fact," she said, passing me by and setting the basket in the dirt underneath the clothesline. She pulled a man's undershirt from a pile of clothes, folded the top over the line and fastened a clothespin on each shoulder.

"Is Cecil really going to shoot Buck?"

"Was you listening to a private conversation?"

"No, ma'am," I said, breaching another convention. To my grandparents' dismay, I addressed all adults as "ma'am" or "sir," regardless of their race. Grandma had scolded Mother about my lapses of correctness on numerous occasions, and had tweaked me directly. In her view, black men and women did not deserve such respectful terms from white people. But Mother responded to her by smiling and saying I was such a polite child, I couldn't help it.

"Not on purpose," I said. "I was just sitting here. I couldn't help hearing."

She lifted a wispy cotton slip and draped it over the line. The slightest bit of breeze picked up the embroidery of its hem.

"I expect he have to, if Mr. Walter say so. I know Cecil'll rather have his hide took off with a switch than have to shoot Buck. That horse be Little Walt's best friend. Him and Chester, that pointer hound he used to have. He the one got killed by wild hogs. Your daddy bawled like a little baby they bring him that dead dog."

In my mind, I saw Daddy sitting atop Buck, his neat, starched khakis the same color as the horse, his rifle slung across his lap, and Chester running around in circles, so excited to be going hunting he was barking and barking and whining. I saw Grandpa too, climbing onto his own horse and carrying his gun in a big soft case with a shoulder strap. I remembered that I couldn't have been more than three or four years old at the time and realized that, one by one, they were disappearing. First Chester, then Daddy. Now Buck.

"Why doesn't Grandpa shoot him?"

Odessa clutched a clothespin between her teeth, and spoke out of one side of her mouth, trying to keep the clothespin from falling out. "Lots of folks don't care much for Mr. Walter, Little Miss. But ain't none of 'em so cold they'd expect Mr. Walter to shoot Little Walt's horse."

I tried to remember when Chester died, but I couldn't. I had never known Daddy to cry, but I had seen Grandpa cry once. It was the night Daddy died, and Grandpa buried his face in his handkerchief. I thought he might drown in the deep, choking sobs. When they at last subsided, he spent the rest of the night in a daze, wandering the hospital room aimlessly.

"Odessa?" Mother rounded the side of the cookhouse. "Did I see Mr. Morton's Lincoln?"

Odessa pulled the last undershirt from the basket and hung it over the line. "Yessum, you sure did," she said. "He in the house."

I wondered if I should tell Mother about Buck, but decided against it. After Daddy's funeral, Grandpa was the one who'd insisted they take Buck up to the place to live, but Mother hadn't objected. Perhaps she was relieved to have another reminder removed to another place.

Mother looked at me strangely. "What are you doing, Chess?"

"Nothing."

"You're filthy. Where on earth have you been?"

"Nowhere," I said, which I felt had been entirely true.

I stood in front of Grandma's pedestal lavatory and turned the ivory handles to stop the flow of water. As the gurgling sound died, Mother's voice echoed down the plastered walls of the hallway. Grandpa's library was just one door down.

I wrapped my fingers in a white hand towel monogrammed with a gold *M* and crept down the hall to the library. Grandpa sat cornered in his creaky, wooden captain's chair, squinting against the glare of Mother's fury. He held a chewed-up toothpick in his teeth, and when he moved his mouth, it switched sides. Mother leaned fully across his desk against the flat palms of her hands. "So help me, God, you brought these people here. You should have realized the impact it would have on them. You should have realized the impact it would have on everybody!"

Grandpa responded by spitting the toothpick into the wastebasket and unfolding his arms. "So quit going out there. For Pete's sake, that'll fix everybody's problems!" He grinned at his own twisted logic, happy to be tormenting her.

"Now you listen to me, Walter Morton," she said, shaking a finger in his direction. "I'm doing my little part to help these people out. I wouldn't even have to come to you for this if you hadn't paid off Judge Pindall so he'd put you in charge of all that land Walt left Chess. I should be making decisions about Chess's property, not you."

Grandpa raised a fat white hand. "You hold on right there, Carrie," he said. "I was doing you a favor. You don't know nothing about running a farm, and you know it."

"Are you out of your mind?"

"Well, you didn't when Walt died. You done pretty good since then, but how was I supposed to know that? I wasn't going to take a chance on you running my granddaughter's place into the ground. And don't you go around saying I bribed anybody. I made a legal campaign contribution to that old man."

Mother stood up straight. "You sent Homer and Cecil and their boys out to his place with four trucks of gravel and a bulldozer. One driveway later, he names you the conservator of Walt's estate."

Grandpa let out a high-pitched cackle, guffawed for a bit, then caught his breath. "If you'll get the hell out of here right now and leave me in peace, Carrie, I'll give 'em an acre. If they can't build a cemetery on an acre of land, they got more problems than I can help 'em with."

Mother crossed her arms. "And clear it for them."

Grandpa waved his hand at her. "Fine. Cleared. Now get out."

She stormed from the room, and I stumbled down the hallway after her, as Grandpa's laughter trailed us through the hall.

Chapter 9

Audrey Ryfle started work at Camp Nine the day that Henry left. Through a sea of people waiting along the railroad tracks, from my vantage point atop a ridge, I saw her blue dress grow larger as she approached a guard tower and pulled a folded letter from her pocket. After she and the soldier at the gate had engaged in some small conversation, he gave her entrance and let his eyes follow her down the dirt road.

As she disappeared behind the Administration Building, I turned my attention to the unfolding scene. A short, dark train sat on the tracks, and Tom, in a uniform of wool pants and a jacket, hat and gloves, stood beside a chicken-wire fence, his eyes obscured in the shadow cast by the morning sun. Even though it was hot as hell's front gate, as Ruby Jean would have said, he didn't seem bothered by the heat. He was on official duty, and his expression betrayed nothing of his thoughts.

A young, smooth-faced soldier with a deep Georgia drawl held a clipboard and mangled the exotic names. One after another, a trail of skinny, lanky boys from Camp Nine made its way up to the platform and climbed on board the train. The atmosphere was solemn, but there were no tears. Mothers wore glasses and sensible shoes, and fathers sweated patiently in their suits and fedoras. When goodbye arrived, the fathers dipped their heads, and the mothers wore a grim line on their faces, but they were framed in bright corsages of paper flowers.

Mrs. Matsui waited at the gate holding Henry's senninbari. Another woman stood next to her, pulling a needle and red thread through the white fabric. She twisted the thread in and around itself until it made a knot, and then snipped it with a small pair of scissors. They exchanged quiet smiles and Mrs. Matsui, the senninbari in her outstretched hands, flew to another waiting friend.

Henry appeared in the distance. With the high cheekbones and glossy black hair of an Indian brave, he looked older than I'd ever seen him. He moved, tall and pale, through a flower garden, brushing through bobbing pink peonies and against rustling asters, down the gravel path to the train. My heart was breaking with each step he took. I couldn't explain it, but in the short time I'd known him, we'd formed a connection deeper than any other I'd ever had. It was more than just our shared interests and the depth of his quiet nature. Although he was years older, I believed I was falling in love with him.

Henry stopped next to his father, who stood motionless in a gray flannel suit, and they passed between them quiet words I couldn't hear. I watched their lips move, first Mr. Matsui and then Henry and then Mr. Matsui again. Henry nodded. Mr. Matsui reached into his pocket and mopped at his forehead with a white handkerchief.

Another neighbor stitched her wish for good fortune into the senninbari. She snipped off her connection to it with the scissors and walked away. Mrs. Matsui looked around the camp grounds, and satisfied that there was no one left who'd not already touched it, clutched the senninbari close to her, and walked with light, quick steps toward the train. She waited, her head low. Henry kissed her on the cheek and slipped the senninbari around his shoulders. Her lips moved. He smiled.

"She put something in the pocket."

The whisper startled me. For a moment, I thought it might have been my imagination, and only then did I realize that I had been holding my breath.

"Watch."

David stood next to me and I breathed again.

Henry reached into the pocket of the white vest and pulled out something small, holding it in his hands.

"What is it?" I asked.

I watched the side of David's face, which was a new story in itself. The morning sun reflected off of his golden skin so much that he glowed. "Cherry blossoms. From our house in California."

He told me the story. To the Japanese, the cherry tree was a symbol of how short and beautiful life was because the blossoms lasted a handful of precious days, then fell to the ground while they were still young and beautiful. Cherry blossoms were kept in wooden boxes for good luck, and it was customary to fill the pockets of the senninbari with the blossoms or locks of hair from mothers and sisters.

Henry bowed to his father. Mr. Matsui waited a minute, then tipped his head in return. For the briefest of moments, Henry looked unbearably sad, but then another boy from the train called to him and he broke free of it. He kissed Mrs. Matsui again, then took off in a run, heading for the train, the tiger on his back leaping along behind. He turned and looked for David. Seeing us both, he waved, then hoisted himself up onto the train.

David left me and ran to the side of the train, shouting at Henry. I wandered to where Tom stood beneath a scraggly cottonwood tree, and leaned against the ragged bark.

Mrs. Matsui took a bright-pink handkerchief from her pocketbook and dabbed at her eye. Mother appeared, it seemed from nowhere, and stood next to her.

The train hissed. Tom took big strides to Mr. and Mrs. Matsui. He said a few words, then picked up Mother's hand and held it, squeezing it without speaking.

The whistle blew. Tom sprinted to the tracks, and as the train groaned and jerked forward, he grabbed the railing and pulled himself aboard. Mother waved goodbye and I did, too, but he couldn't see me. He held onto the railing with two hands, and leaned back.

Mother put her arm around Mrs. Matsui, and, together, they watched the train pull out.

I ran to the edge of the tracks. Henry passed before me, his blank eyes staring straight at Camp Nine as he moved away, as if he could see something that the rest of us couldn't. Then he looked at me, and in that moment, I was as sorry that he was leaving us as I was of anything that had ever happened. I held my hand up in front of me, and the breeze pushed against my flat palm. I meant for it to be a wave, but it looked like I was telling him to stop.

Henry held up his hand and mirrored mine. As the train rolled past, the whistle blew again. He twisted round to face McHenry and then he was gone.

It was as dark inside the store as was Mother's disposition, now that Henry had left for Camp Shelby. She hadn't said a word as we'd driven away, lost to her thoughts and, for once, not in any mood to talk about anyone's troubles. Our stopping at Mr. Gilwell's mercantile seemed to be more an act of habit than her conscious choice.

The ceiling fan wobbled above our heads, providing no comfort, but merely moving the hot air around us in lazy, humid circles. Mr. Gilwell was in the back, tugging to tighten the ropes of a mail sack. "Morning, Carrie."

Mother made her way toward him. "Morning," she said blandly, and leaned on the worn, wooden counter. "Let me ask you a question, Jim. If somebody put you in prison even though you'd done nothing wrong, do you think you'd hold a grudge?"

Mr. Gilwell looked up, surprised that she'd ask a question with such an obvious answer. "You bet I would." With a sucking sound, he slapped a rubber stamp on a letter.

"Do you know," she said, "that not twenty minutes ago, about a hundred of those Japanese boys over at Camp Nine got on a train and left for Camp Shelby, Mississippi, so they could fight in the US Army?"

His large eyes blinked behind his thick glasses. "You don't say," he said, tossing the letter into a canvas bag.

She nodded thoughtfully.

He squinted his oversized eyes. "Why would they do something like that, Carrie?"

"Because they're Americans, Jim," she said, pulling herself from the counter and sauntering away, her hands straining the pockets of her bright cotton dress. "But for some reason, they're the only ones we're making prove it."

The spring on the screen door cried out and the wood frame bounced hard two or three times, which happened whenever someone had carelessly opened it too wide, causing it to slam shut. The shadow of a group of people of varied sizes stood out against the white hot daylight glinting off the hood of a beat-up pickup.

Mother raised her eyebrows.

Mr. Ryfle ambled through the aisles, along with his wife and six of their nine children, including Jesse. "Jim Gilwell!" he bellowed.

"In the back, Hammond!"

The Ryfle children roamed the store like a pack of loose dogs, while Mrs. Ryfle held the youngest one.

"We come for the mail," Mr. Ryfle said.

"Not in yet," Mr. Gilwell said. "That gov'ment train blocked the track. Mail train'll be late."

Mr. Ryfle moved a chaw of chewing tobacco from one cheek to the other. A brown trickle trailed his chin. "What the hell gov'ment train?"

Mr. Gilwell picked up a package and placed it on a scale. "Army train. According to Miss Morton, it's carrying Jap boys to Camp Shelby."

Mr. Ryfle lifted a tin can to his face and squirted a brown stream from his mouth. "Them foreigners don't belong in DeSoto County. They need to ship the whole damn bunch of 'em back to Jay-pan," he said.

"No sir. We need them boys to fight for us," Mr. Gilwell said. "Don't you think so, Carrie?"

"You're absolutely right, Jim," she said.

Mr. Ryfle snorted like a bull. "I got a idee what them fellows think of the US of A, and so do you, Jim," he said, ignoring Mother altogether. "I know for a fact they're plotting attacks on that railroad line out to the river port. Remember Pearl Harbor."

Where Mr. Ryfle had heard that bit of nonsense, we could only imagine. A new rumor surfaced every week about some imagined enemy subversion. Mother's unscientific theory was that Mr. Ryfle started half of them himself to fan hysteria to recruit the poor whites to his fledgling Klan chapter, about which we'd continued to hear rumblings. But Mr. Gilwell, who intercepted every story that made the rounds, had become immune to the gossip.

"This country's made up of lots of different people, Hammond," Mr. Gilwell said. "Everybody here's parents done come from somewhere else. Even yours."

"My momma and daddy come here from Mississippi," Mr. Ryfle barked and Mrs. Ryfle snickered. He cut his eyes sharply at Mother, but she regarded him coolly.

"You know what I mean, Hammond," Mr. Gilwell said. "Even if I was just a little one, I remember your daddy like it was yesterday. Irish as a sack of potatoes. Them Japanese folks from California is just the same as you and me."

"Like hell, Jim Gilwell, and you know it," Mr. Ryfle said.

Mother shook her head lightly and lifted the top off the cookie jar.

Mrs. Ryfle picked up a can of potted ham with her hefty paw. "I hear they get real beef over there at Camp Nine," she said. "I ain't got no beef but what I kin slaughter m'self."

Mother reached in the cookie jar and pulled out two lemon cookies and handed them to me. "Ethel, you've never eaten store-bought beef in your life, so why are you complaining?"

Mrs. Ryfle puffed herself up like a hog and cocked her ugly head at Mother. "Well, I never!" She began to say more, but Mr. Ryfle's strategic jab in her ribs silenced her.

Mrs. Ryfle released some of her air and batted her eyes at Mother. "All I'm saying is, they got it better over there than we do. It ain't fair they got food and electricity and such when the gov'ment don't do nothing for us but 'cept take tax money." She released the potted ham back to the shelf.

"You still got your home, Ethel," Mother said, her voice rising. "And your way of life. Let somebody come take that from you, and then you tell me if it's worth trading for all the corn you can stuff in your greedy mouth."

I followed her as she stormed the exit. She was halfway outside when she stopped abruptly and turned. "And then you also tell me if you'd send your boys off to fight and die for a government that would do that to you."

Mrs. Ryfle stared at us, stunned.

Mother faced her fiercely. "You hear me, Ethel?" Then she let the screen slam loudly, which she'd always before been too much of a lady to do.

Col. Tom Jefferies spent more time at Camp Nine than his duties required. As a commander at the largest military installation for hundreds of miles, there were likely more pressing things that required his attention in Mississippi. But his presence became so familiar at Camp Nine that it seemed more unusual when he was gone. He would appear on a Monday and his stays numbered anywhere from two days to a week or more. From my perch in the art room, I often saw him strolling the grounds, visiting with Mr. Hayashida in the vegetable garden, or riding in the passenger seat of a jeep driven by a corporal. Whenever he passed the soldiers, they saluted and stood at attention, and my ability to have his interest whenever I liked and enjoy his unguarded company made me believe that there was something special and privileged about me.

The house in which he lived while at Camp Nine was a simple

farm dwelling. A wide porch stretched across the front, and there sat two rocking chairs, which Mother had covered with striped cushions. It wasn't fair that he had to be away from home so much, she had told me as she affixed the final piece of deep-green grosgrain with her sewing machine. His house here would be all cold and lonely if it weren't for us, she'd insisted, her head bent low while she guided fabric through her sewing machine.

Once he had installed Henry and his buddies at Camp Shelby, he'd returned. His weeklong visit had suited all of us nicely, especially Gretchen, the German shepherd. She was napping on the sliver of carpet that served as a welcome mat by his front door.

Mother's chair creaked back and forth. Her shoes sat on the wood floor, and her soft, bare feet, propped on the railing, caught the warm wind that blew across the cotton field, rippling the white bolls. A glass of iced tea melted on the table at her elbow. Her eyes were closed. Against the side of the porch, the gleaming undersides of the leaves of a silver-leaf maple fluttered noisily like the charms of a bracelet.

I sat on the floor and ran my fingers through Gretchen's thick fur. Her heavy tail thumped so hard it shook the floorboards as Tom's dark form grew larger in the interior hallway. Gretchen pulled herself up slowly, her curved haunches stretching, and moved away from the screen door as it opened.

Tom carried a duffle bag over his shoulder and a suit bag in his hand. He heaved the duffle bag from his back, and it thudded to the floor.

Mother's eyes opened, but only half-way. Her peacock-blue dress cascaded over the side of the rocking chair, her skin browned from the summer sun. "Is it time already?" she asked.

Tom draped the suit bag over his shoulder. "Tell me I don't have to go," he said.

She looked far across the field where the army train sat on the tracks, and began to hum the song they listened to in the evenings on the phonograph, "I'll Never Smile Again."

The breeze died down and gave way to a sultry stillness. The silver-leaf maple fell silent.

He stood looking at her. She stopped humming and turned her gaze toward him lazily as if she were dreaming him up from thin air. "They're waiting for you, Tom," she said.

He sucked in a deep breath and held it. "I know," he said, exhaling. He held out his hand to her, and she lifted the back of it to her face, sliding it across her skin and closing her eyes.

Without another word from either of them, he picked up the duffle bag and walked slowly to the jeep and threw his bag in the back. He started the engine and drove straight away from us.

I felt as though the air had grown heavy, as if a storm were coming. But the sun shone clear and bright as it dipped down over the horizon, blazing orange around us as Tom's jeep motored toward the tracks.

It was only by happenstance that I learned how David managed to get past our house without us seeing him. A small trail, rarely used, ran along the boundary of Grandpa's property and skirted the backside of our barn. It was directly accessible from the northern guard tower of Camp Nine. If David slipped unnoticed under the barbed wire, all he had to do was cross the highway, and disappear into the tall weeds that surrounded the trail. I discovered his route one morning when I happened to be out back of our house in the garden that Ruby Jean tended, gathering okra before it got to be long and rangy, and therefore inedible. I never liked the slimy stuff, but Mother craved Ruby Jean's fresh okra, coated in cornmeal and flour and fried crispy. I stood in the heat of the morning underneath the towering plants, and snipped the pods with a small pair of shears, trying to avoid the stinging hairs that lined the stalks.

The bark of a distant dog got my attention. Beyond the barn, a cap bobbed over the tops of the weeds. I watched from the safety of the okra forest as a dark form carrying a black guitar case emerged onto the gravel road and cut through the woods toward Black Bayou. I knew from the familiar lope that it was David. I also knew that I had to follow him, although if Ruby Jean caught me she'd have my hide. I dropped my basket on the ground, pushed my way from the cultivated jungle, and sprinted along after him.

I crossed the bayou bridge and crept quietly down the path to the tenant houses, careful to avoid snapping twigs or rustling stray branches. I took the fork in the path toward Willie's. It was the only place David would be headed.

I paused at the edge of the woods and listened. Two voices spoke too quietly for me to hear. I would have to get closer.

Lush pomegranate bushes ringed Willie's tiny house, but they were low to the ground. The multiple slender trunks of a crape myrtle, not yet in bloom, sprang from the weeds near the porch. It wasn't much, but it was somewhere to hide. Bright-green grasshoppers skipped along the dewy grass in advance of my footsteps. Willie's and David's voices became clearer as I neared the open window of Willie's living room and squeezed myself into the smooth reaches of the young tree.

There was a muffled cough, and as notes flew rapidly from a guitar, Willie spit out quick words in a gravelly voice, much different from the levee camp holler he had sung to me before. "Well, if I had my way, if I had my way. Well, if I had my way, I'd burn that building down." A second guitar started in, in perfect harmony.

"How do you *do* that?" David asked, the second guitar still sounding. It was then that I realized I was hearing Willie's signature double-guitar sound.

Willie stopped. "Boy, I can't explain it. It just be, that's all. Now you try."

Competent, but less expert, notes floated through the window. Feet tapped in time on the wood floor. David missed a lick, and cursed. Willie laughed.

David sang. "Well, if I had my way, if I had my way. Well, if I had my way, I'd burn that building down."

Willie stopped him. "That's alright, boy, but you ain't feeling it. It ain't 'bout how many notes you can juke out that box. You got to feel the blues. Try it again."

David ran through the same notes. They were all there, but something was missing.

"Don't be running all up and down it. Stick in them same few notes. You got to concentrate it. That the hypnotism you need. You get that hypnotize going, you in the blues. You cain't be thinking in your head. Get lost in it."

David tried again, this time repeating the riffs so tightly it formed a cyclical, spellbinding wall of sound.

"That's better, that's better. Now bring it on home. Your woman done run off, and the boss man working you to death, and he ain't paying you. And boy, you got nowhere to turn. Cain't go to church and pray over it none, 'cause preacher the one that done took your gal!"

They rocked with laughter, and whatever Willie had to teach him, David had suddenly grasped it. His notes took on their best quality, coming more fluid and fast. Relaxed and loose, David and Willie sang in unison, their voices pinched and tight through their noses, Willie sometimes dipping into a lower register below David and rounding out a melody. Then Willie picked up another guitar part and it sounded for all the world as if an entire band was playing.

They stopped from time to time to switch songs and trade stories. My legs tired, and I sank into the soft grass to listen, no longer afraid that someone might see me there. I was in a new world, one that existed just next to mine, and yet had been hidden from me. But I didn't have the courage to walk in the front door. I stayed for a while, then, as their session wound down, I crept back across Willie's yard, slinking like a thief through the woods toward home.

Chapter 10

My Aunt Margaret's black Chrysler, parked in Grandma's driveway, was girded in shiny chrome. Margaret, my father's only sibling, betrayed none of her country upbringing. In her college days, she'd been the president of Chi Omega at the University of Arkansas, a homecoming queen, and eventually a bearer of what Mother called an "MRS. degree."

Neither Mother nor I cared a bit for either Margaret or her only child, Babe, but we were compelled to be polite whenever we were forced to endure their company. Privately, Mother thought Aunt Margaret a social climber and a snob, although she didn't use those terms directly. Instead, she derided certain of Margaret's actions which illustrated her faults, such as her conversion to the Episcopal Church simply to improve her social standing and her pushing her insurance agent husband to the brink of financial ruin so that she could enjoy a Tudor style home in the elegant Little Rock neighborhood of Pulaski Heights.

Standing beneath Grandma's oaks, Margaret wore a smart linen city suit, high-heeled shoes, and a hat with cherries on top. She held her square alligator pocketbook in her white-gloved hands, trading urgent whispers with Grandma, suspending them as I approached.

Babe's blond waves bounced up and down, and she clapped her

fleshy hands at the palms. Her excitement was over a calico kitten, which was pouncing on a ball as if it were a live mouse.

"Chess!" Babe squealed when she saw me, not because she liked me, but because I was someone to whom she could flaunt her new kitten.

Margaret tucked her pocketbook under her arm and began peeling her gloves from her fingers, irritated that I had arrived. "Chess, come see Babe's new kitten. Isn't it just darling?"

It was darling, I had to give her that. I supposed it had come from a litter that had escaped Odessa's shovel. I'd seen Odessa discover a cat giving birth and bury the kittens alive just as they emerged. She claimed it was better for them that way, but I suspected it was only better for Odessa, as it was one less thing for her to care for. Sometimes the cats were too smart for her, and had their kittens under houses or barns where she couldn't find them until they were too old for her to dispatch.

"I've named her Snowball," Babe said. My first thought was that Snowball was a name for white cats, and my second was that its name ought to be "Lucky." But, as Mother had prompted me, I kept my thoughts to myself, knelt down and picked up the ball.

Babe crouched next to me, her pink taffeta dress brushing against my plain cotton pants. My scuffed Buster Browns looked poor and worn next to her shiny, white patent-leather buckle shoes. "Come here, Snowball," she said. The kitten stopped her play and trained her big orange eyes on her new mistress.

Margaret opened her pocketbook and tossed her gloves inside. "Girls, why don't y'all take Snowball over to the magnolia tree," she said in the tight voice she used when she tried to pass herself off as a pleasant person.

"Okay!" Babe sang. "Let's go, Snowball!" She scooped up the cat, cradling her like a baby. Snowball flopped her flaccid head over the side and peered at me upside down. Babe carried her to the giant tree and placed her in the waxy, brown leaves. I picked up a dried seed pod, pulled out the bright, red seeds and began tossing them on the ground. Snowball batted her tiny paws at them as they landed.

"Don't let her eat those," Babe said, queen again. "They're probably poisonous."

"I won't," I said.

Grandma and Margaret drew together, their backs to us, and talked low. Margaret held her hand up alongside her face, but her voice carried. "He's originally from Little Rock," she said. "His father was a state senator for years. I think he was high up at the bank or something."

Grandma twisted her neck briefly to check on us. "Who is *she*?" she asked.

Margaret fluffed the netting on her hat. "She was Maxine Meador. You know, the Meador Furniture fortune."

Grandma murmured as if the very thought of someone else's fortune was tasty.

"I don't think you ever met her," Margaret continued, "but she was in my sorority, a year behind me. We knew them when he was stationed in Little Rock. Right before he was sent to Camp Shelby. And they have three little children. All girls."

Grandma lowered her chin and raised her eyebrows in the direction of our house. "Well," she said, "it's certainly not his fault."

Margaret gathered her lips together as if she were afraid something was going to fly into her mouth. "It's one thing for her to go around, acting all progressive. But now this."

Grandma stuck her nose in the air. I've seen starlings fight with each other. They crane their necks out with their beaks straight up in the air and poke randomly at the sky. Grandma and Margaret were dead ringers.

They were asinine to think that I wouldn't know what they were talking about. Now, as a mother myself, I'm enraged by their recklessness to have been carrying on such gossip in my presence. Mother's assessments of both Margaret and Grandma were correct. They couldn't have cared less about us. They would not bring themselves to sympathize with the lonely widow and the fatherless child. We were just fodder for scandal, the outsiders, and beneath their sensibilities.

My ankles hurt, so I rearranged myself and propped my knees in the dirt, digging them in deeper on purpose, soiling the fabric of my trousers with the rich earth, defiant by proxy against their sterile, merciless ideals.

Babe chattered beside me, but I couldn't keep my eyes off Margaret's sharp features. As Snowball batted her razor claws at my finger, I tried to imagine life with Margaret as my mother. The thought terrified me. At the time, I was unable or unwilling to judge my mother's choices. I only knew that I loved her, that if I could choose to, I would be her, and that no matter how fine Margaret might have thought her life to be, she could only pale beside Carolina Morton.

As I stood in the gravel just inside the grounds of Camp Nine, purple martins made figure eights up in the sky above me, so high I could barely see them.

"Chess, hold these, will you?" Mother said, handing me the two heavy cans of varnish she'd obtained from Mr. Gilwell for Mr. Hayashida. She leaned two stretched canvases against her leg, slammed the trunk of the Buick, and picking up a canvas in each hand, walked away down the sidewalk toward the community center. As I followed her, a bulletin board announced a high school dance and a Boy Scout campout. A girls' chorus floated through an open window. In the field outside Camp Nine, a crop duster droned upward like a giant horsefly, then wound down out of our hearing.

"Mama?"

"What, honey?"

"Do you know a lady named Maxine Meador?"

Mother missed a step. She paused briefly, then resumed walking. "Why do you ask?"

My heart beat rapidly. "Grandma and Aunt Margaret were talking about her and they said she lives at Camp Shelby. They said they're worried about her."

Mother bit her lip as if she wanted to respond, but she took her time. "As a matter of fact, Chess, I do know her," she said after a moment. "Maxine Meador is now Maxine Jefferies. She's Colonel Tom's wife."

As we neared the Administration Building, Mother shook her head. "Your Aunt Margaret is a troublemaker of the first order. I'm sure Maxine Jefferies is just fine, and Margaret is wasting lots of her precious time worrying about nothing."

She'd barely gotten the words out when the double front doors burst open. Four MPs spilled toward us, their helmets pulled close to their eyes, hustling a handcuffed prisoner down the narrow sidewalk, which could hardly accommodate two people. With no word of apology, their momentum diverted us from our path and knocked a canvas from Mother's hand. Even though his fedora was pulled tightly down over his face, I saw in an instant that the man being dragged against his will was Mr. Matsui.

Mother turned as they passed, her mouth wide open as if there would have been words coming out if she could only think of something to say. But the men were gone in a flash, disappeared around the corner of the Administration Building, toward the entrance to Camp Nine.

The crop duster buzzed as it made its next turn over the field. The girls' chorus paused, and the music teacher rustled sheet music. The purple martins dipped and weaved. The hurried group that had moved through us made ripples in all the ordinary world that was going on around us, like a motorboat on a still lake.

"Mama?"

She stared at the space where they had traveled, not hearing me.

———

Despite her vigorous cross-examination, Mother's long-distance call to Tom yielded only this: Mr. Matsui's answers to "the questions" had placed him under suspicion. Now it was apparent that the questions Mr. Hayashida had told us about that day months ago were more important than he had let on.

As restrictions on the residents of the relocation camps began to ease, all adult residents, men and women, citizens and non-citizens, were required to fill out what was innocently enough titled "Application for Leave Clearance." Most questions were routine, mundane even, such as their names and ages. But two questions stood out, and they were two questions that would not only divide families and tear apart communities—they would provide the means through which men like Mr. Matsui would find themselves branded disloyal.

It was apparently of no consequence that neither Mr. Matsui nor the hundreds of other residents who were forced to answer the questionnaire had even requested leave clearance. Mother pondered aloud whether the whole thing had been no more than a scheme by the government to force the Japanese to pledge their allegiance, something she considered not only illegal but immoral.

Her argument with Tom, at least the side of it which I heard, was fierce. Whether she was right or wrong about the reasons behind the questions, she believed that Tom knew more than he was telling her, and that he owed not only her, but the Matsuis, an explanation. What he replied, I didn't know, but the explanation either didn't come or it wasn't enough to satisfy her.

The only thing that was certain was that Mr. Matsui was gone. Tom would not tell Mother where he was—it was classified information for now, he said. He begged her patience, promising that information would come soon enough, but she told him this was a matter of more than military protocol. The conversation petered out into a few moments of tense silence, then a clipped goodbye.

She'd barely slammed down the receiver when a sharp rapping at the back door brought a new set of problems.

"Miz Morton?"

It was Hammond Ryfle.

Mother and I exchanged glances. "What the hell does he want?" she asked under her breath. Mr. Ryfle made himself scarce around our house, and his appearance never heralded good news. Mother wove through the kitchen toward the back porch, and I followed along several safe steps behind her.

Mr. Ryfle tapped his boots on the step to clear them of mud and helped himself inside the screen door.

Mother stuffed her hands in the pockets of her apron. "Good morning, Hammond."

He swept the cap from his head. "Howdy, Miz Morton."

"Is there a problem?"

She was unwilling to entertain pleasantries with him and her directness unsettled him. "Well, no'm. I mean, yessum. A little bit."

"What is it?"

As Mr. Ryfle reported that he was again delayed in clearing her hundred acres, she pushed her hands farther into her pockets until the straps cut into her shoulders. She said nothing, but frowned, and he shifted anxiously, as if he wished he were somewhere else. "Mr. Ryfle," she said at length, "I bought that acreage two years ago on your assurance that it would not be a problem to clear it. I not only sunk good money into it only to find out from you that you've changed your mind about its quality and believe it's unsuitable for cotton, I also have to pay annual taxes on a swamp that you cannot find the time to clear." Her words were directed at Mr. Ryfle, but her tone was left over from her futile conversation with Tom.

He twisted his cap in his hands. "Yessum, I know that. You done fussed at me afore 'bout that."

"It is already July. It may be too late to cultivate it, but I want it cleared. In fact, I had expected you to be working on it already."

The problem, it seemed once again, lay not at Mr. Ryfle's feet. The armed forces had depleted his workforce, and he was left with only his younger children. And as Mother knew, he continued with undisguised irk, his girl, Audrey, was employed during the day with government work.

Mother sighed and relaxed her hands. Mr. Ryfle slapped his hat on his head and took a step forward. "You can blame it on Hilter," he cackled, as if he were delivering a poorly timed punch line to a political joke.

Mother set her jaw. "Hitler."

He cocked his head. "Come again?"

"Hitler. The man's name is Adolf Hitler."

The lines of his mouth settled into an unpleasant grin. "Yessum," he said. "I reckon you know more about them foreigners what's responsible for this war better'n I do." He touched his fingers to the tip of his cap. "Good day to you, Miz Morton."

She waited until the door slammed and he was off the steps and down the path. "The old fool," she said, the sharpest insult in her arsenal.

But if there was one thing that was squarely within my mother's nature, it was this: A handful of petty troubles might worry her to her sickbed, but an armload of real troubles spurred her out the door and into action. She peered through the kitchen window into Ruby Jean's garden until she'd formulated a plan.

By the time she reached for the car keys, I was already waiting by the door.

The letters on the frosted glass panel spelled "SUPERINTENDENT." David stood behind me, restlessly turning the insides of his pockets out and then back in again. Mother placed her hand on the brass doorknob and twisted it, and we passed through the doorway into a bright, open office area with a weathered rug, chairs, an assortment of desks, and some filing cabinets. Four iron desk fans whirred, forcing the hot air into a vortex in the center of the room.

Miss Lilly McGehee, a small, gray-haired lady imported from Louisiana, sat sideways at a large desk, her fingers crooked and poised at the keys of a decrepit typewriter. At the far corner of the room, Audrey Ryfle leaned against an open filing cabinet, five graceful, ivory fingers clutching a sheaf of papers, the other five wedging open a space between cardboard files.

Their heads swiveled upward as Mother, David, and I walked into the room. Audrey gave a brief start upon seeing us. I knew that neither my arrival nor Mother's would have caused Audrey a second thought, so I instinctively peeked at David and caught him pretending to be unconcerned. They were already acquainted, it seemed.

"Afternoon, Miss Morton," Miss McGehee said.

"Afternoon, Lilly. Audrey."

Audrey returned her attention to her task and murmured.

"May we see Mr. Brown?" Mother asked.

"Of course, honey, he's in there. Go on in," Miss McGehee said, waving her birdlike hand toward a heavy door.

"David," Mother said, "why don't you wait out here while I talk to Mr. Brown? Chess, you can come with me."

David took a seat in a row of tacked leather chairs along the wall and picked up a copy of *The Bugler,* the Camp Nine newspaper. Mother approached the door and raised her knuckles to knock, but paused. She turned back to David. "Do you know Audrey Ryfle?" she asked.

If David and Audrey had built a brick wall between them, they couldn't have tried any harder to hide the fact that not only did they, indeed, know each other, they would prefer that the rest of us not be aware of it. David sat up straighter. "No, ma'am." He ran his fingers through his crown of hair and smoothed it flat, although a thick lock around his temple popped up straight.

"Audrey," she said, "this is David Matsui. His parents are friends of ours."

"Yes, ma'am," Audrey said.

"You two are about the same age, I think," Mother said absently, too preoccupied to notice what was clearly in front of her.

David stole a furtive glance from behind the newspaper, but it wasn't directed at me.

Mr. Howard E. D. Brown, the superintendent of Camp Nine, was pasty and plump in the middle, evidence of a lifetime spent behind a desk. Looming over his dark suit, bow tie, and horn-rimmed glasses was a portrait of FDR. In front of him, his nameplate glinted in the slatted light pouring through the venetian blinds. Maps of DeSoto County and Camp Nine commandeered the wall space behind him.

"Education is very important to the Japanese," Mr. Howard E. D. Brown said.

Mother's hackles were raised. Mr. Brown might as well have told Thomas Edison that light was important. "I understand their culture as well as you do. But many of these people have farm experience."

Mother had come to Mr. Brown only as a courtesy. After fuming about the twin distractions of Tom Jefferies's call and Hammond Ryfle's visit, she'd bustled to the telephone, and called Tom back. There was something he could do, after all.

But Mr. Brown wasn't moved. "I was brought here from Philadelphia, Mrs. Morton. We didn't have any farm children in my district."

"The schedule for the boys from Camp Nine could be the same as it is for the levee children at the Kimble School," she said patiently, as if Mr. Brown were a child who needed concepts to be broken into small bits. "They could work this summer, and when school starts, before or after school and on the weekends. I'm sure my farm isn't the only one that can use additional labor. And some of these families might welcome the extra income."

Mr. Brown fiddled with his tie. "We've had some men approved to leave for the sugar beet harvest in Montana, but security was high. How are you planning to guard these folks?"

Mother stiffened. "Mr. Brown," she said curtly, "I don't operate the Cummins State Farm. These people are law-abiding American citizens. If I believed there were any danger whatsoever, I wouldn't be here asking you to allow them access to my property." She fingered her earring. "And I want to start by hiring David Matsui."

Mr. Brown's eyebrows shot up over the top of his horn-rims. "Absolutely not. Hiroshi Matsui was a problem."

While she'd been unable to take her frustrations out on Tom and Mr. Ryfle, the hapless Mr. Brown was unlucky enough to be sitting across from her. "I'm not asking you to allow Hiroshi Matsui to leave Camp Nine. That would be quite impossible since he's already been handcuffed and dragged off to God knows where for refusing to answer two simple questions to the satisfaction of Henry L. Stimson."

Mr. Brown shifted in his chair as if he felt a pain, but Mother was on a roll and there was no stopping her. Besides, she'd already set the wheels in motion behind Mr. Brown's ample back.

But just as she seemed as if she might spring from the chair and wring his neck, she simmered down and took a deep breath. "Mr. Brown," she said evenly, "I have a business to run, and every able-bodied boy of legal age has joined the army or the navy or the marines and is now at least five thousand miles away from the trees I need cleared and the stumps I need pulled and the chunks I need picked up and piled up and burned. The families in this camp have lost everything, including their ability to earn a livelihood. Sakura Matsui's husband is gone and her oldest is off training in Mississippi. These people need to work and they know how to work and I intend to employ them."

He removed his glasses and rubbed them fiercely with a handkerchief. "I don't think that's going to be possible, Mrs. Morton," he said. "The War Relocation Authority . . ."

"I will get the WRA's permission whether you like it or not," she said, standing.

He stood as well, confounded. He held his glasses and peered at her oddly, as if he couldn't understand why he couldn't see her clearly. He abruptly popped his glasses onto his nose and stuffed the handkerchief in his pocket. "Why, I don't believe you're going to be able to get it," he said. "I just don't see how."

Her hand sliced the space between them and stalled. "Good day, Mr. Brown."

He paused for a moment, then reluctantly touched the tips of her fingers, giving them a lukewarm squeeze. "Good day, Mrs. Morton."

She opened the door and sailed like a fast, smooth ship into the reception area, where David sat slumped in his seat, his long legs crossed at the ankles and his big feet thrust out into the middle of the room. He sat up straight as Mother approached.

"David," she said, "I want you to remember something. Leaving the camp is a privilege that you have to treat with the proper respect."

"Yes, ma'am," he said briskly, leaping to his feet.

"Do we understand each other?"

"Yes, ma'am."

It was a warning which David would have done better to heed.

Mother didn't dare assume assistance from Mr. Ryfle. While his shortage of able-bodied farm boys and girls posed a real impediment to him, she wisely understood that he would oppose her plan to employ Japanese men and boys on her farm. She needed, then, an ally, and the logical choice was the gentle farmer from the Monterey Bay, Edo Hayashida. He'd already transformed Camp Nine from a dead swamp into deep trails of abundant vegetables that stretched all the way to the trees at the edge of the camp, and, when she posed her request to him at Camp Nine that afternoon, he was delighted to marshal a team.

He began by leading us on a tour of his miraculous garden, which fanned out before us like Joseph's cloak. Planting his feet in the thick Delta mud, known locally as buckshot dirt, he pointed a crooked finger toward the tree line. "The bayou is that way," he said. "We had two problems." He turned and indicated toward the other direction. "The first thing is that that area flooded." He took a few steps and stood on the edge of a shallow ditch. "And the second thing is that this area was too dry."

Mother walked to the ditch and surveyed it both ways. "So you've got drainage from the swampy area and bayou to irrigate this section?" she asked.

"That's how we did it in Castroville," he said. The furrows of his face gathered at his cheeks and spread out from there. "The white people didn't think anything could grow on that dried-up old land, so they let us have it. If they had thought it had any value, they would never have let us get our paws on it."

"We have a lot in common, Edo," Mother said. "Two outcasts." She placed her hands on her hips, taking in the wide circle around her. "The only reason you're standing on this land right now is because Walter Morton didn't think he'd be able to get any yield out of it."

Mr. Hayashida kicked a clod of buckshot with the toe of his rubber boot. "Oh," he murmured, "this is good earth. Very good earth." He picked up a handful and broke it between his fingers. It fell to the ground in tiny balls like BB gun pellets. "You just got to work *with* it. You can't make it into something it's not. Kind of like people, right?"

Her eyes crinkled in the sun. "Very much like people."

We moved on to the edge of the field, where tomatoes, carrots, peppers, peas, potatoes, okra, and spinach baked in the sun like multicolored ribbon candy.

"The land here is very unusual," he said, stopping where the brown earth ended and the colored rows began. "Doesn't like to retain the water. Wants to always send the water somewhere else, so you get flooding all the time. I think I understand it, though." He surveyed the bright distance toward the levee as the cicadas tuned up in the low branches of the trees that surrounded us. "That river over there is the mightiest river in the world. It wouldn't do for there to be just any dirt around here. The dirt here must have its own strong personality. It won't back down to the river. It won't back down to men. You have to understand it and work with it. Not against it."

It would be many years before America would become accustomed to talk like that, the idea that the world at large is alive, not just something to plow up and chop down and bend to our will. But they were the same sentiments I'd heard from Ruby Jean and her family. Despite the atrocities they were forced to commit against the earth with our newfangled chemicals and poisons, they maintained a reverence and respect for nature that went far beyond our desire for dominance over what we could never truly hope to tame.

Mr. Hayashida grinned. "We'll fix your problem, Carrie. We got some good, strong boys here. Right now they got nothing useful to do. Having a job will do them good."

Chapter 11

Henry had been gone for two months, but it had seemed like two years. He came to me at night, in simple dreams where we talked again of the things we loved. The gulf between our ages kept romance out of my head during the day, but in my subconscious, in sleep where I had no control over my feelings, I entertained notions of something more than friendship. The dreams lingered long after I awoke, leaving me vaguely sad and lost, as if it would have been better if he'd never come at all. What role I believed Henry played in my life, I don't know. I had hardly known him. But I couldn't help but grieve the loss of his company, and when I learned that he was coming home on leave, it felt like a holiday.

The reason for the special visit home was that there was trouble at Camp Shelby. The segregated Japanese American fighting force assembled as the 442nd Regimental Combat Team wasn't progressing as planned. The problem was that although to the white officers the soldiers all looked roughly the same, they simply weren't.

At the outbreak of the war, military service was denied the Japanese Americans. Gradually, it was opened to them, but first to those living in the Hawaiian Islands. Soon after, Japanese Americans living on the mainland were permitted in the 442nd. But while the mainland soldiers might have come from different states and cities, they shared one shameful struggle—their families were in prison in the interior. The Hawaiians, a boisterous, scrappy bunch, either didn't know that fact, or didn't understand its significance in making the mainlanders so reserved and frugal. They perceived the West Coast soldiers as arrogant and snobbish, and the inevitable fights were bloody and threatening the existence of the 442nd. Something had to be done. The Hawaiians needed to see Rook.

The evening sun glinted off the tin roof of the store and seared through my eyes. I sat on our front steps, a gentle sweat forming under my arms and around my waist, and stared toward the empty road, waiting for the troop train to arrive at the depot. It seemed as though we'd not felt a breeze since June, and I wanted so badly to be pretty when the soldiers arrived. But I'd been there for over an hour, and the train was late.

My new organdy dress scratched against my cotton slip as I rearranged myself on the top concrete step. Now that I was thirteen, Ruby Jean no longer washed my hair for me in the sink. Mother had allowed me to grow out my poorly cut pageboy, if I promised to keep it clean, and it had grown long over the summer. Now more like Mother's, it curled into deep, dark waves in the August heat. I was by then a head taller than she was, and she'd relented on a little bit of lipstick, just for that special occasion. When I appeared in my blue dress with the swiss dot overlay, Ruby Jean laid her hand over her heart and said she wished Little Walt were here to see his little girl all grown up. But I felt unsure in my shoes, which had the slightest heel, and my knees were still scabby from playing outside.

The whistle blew, startling me from my reverie. I scrambled to my feet and called out that I was leaving, not caring if Mother heard me. Without waiting for her response, I wobbled across the road to the store, reaching the platform of the station just as the train came around the bend. A brakeman stood to the side of the tracks, swinging his light. As the train slowed down on its approach, the bell clanged, and the train came to a great, creaking stop.

A dozen MPs streamed out onto the platform and formed a solid line, standing between the tracks and me. They held their rifles and shifted their weight back and forth from foot to foot. Barely able to peer through their ranks, I craned my neck to see between the starched shirts and black arm-bands. I didn't know what I would see, but I anxiously waited.

A few tense moments passed with no activity. Then a sea of khaki stirred behind the windows, and I heard happy, barking voices, young men trading words in English that didn't make sense to me. Dillies and dames and heebie-jeebies.

A tiny, brown-skinned boy with a crew cut poked his head from the train and stepped forward, but then stopped abruptly. His eyes grew wide, and his mouth slammed shut. Two other boys tried to leave the car, but they bumped into him as he blocked the exit.

"Christ, Louie, come on!" one of them insisted.

Louie stood still on the train steps, holding onto the railing as if he were afraid that he might fall off. "Goddamn," he muttered, looking around at the station and the store.

"Let us off, lizard!" a voice yelled from inside the train.

Louie, whose uniform read "L. Yamaguchi," stepped onto the platform in a trance. Others behind him followed, but when they reached the platform and got their first glimpse of Rook, each one fell silent, until nearly a hundred Japanese boys in army uniforms were standing speechless next to the train.

Thirty to forty of the boys from Camp Nine, including Henry, unfolded themselves from the train, laughing and talking. If his uniform had not read "H. Matsui," I would not have recognized him. Since he'd spent his days in the sun, instead of cooped up in a library, his skin was tanned. His uniform fit tightly across his shoulders, which were much broader than his waist. He jumped lightly onto the platform, his heavy boots thudding on the wood. He stood tall among the others, many of them no bigger that the boys below me in school.

Henry slapped one of the short fellows on the back. "What'd I tell you, Buddahead?"

A burst of laughter skittered among the group. The short soldier, a Hawaiian, or Buddahead, as they had come to be called by the mainlanders, reached in his pocket and fished out a pack of cigarettes, shaking it, and pulling out a single cigarette with his teeth. "What a dump," he said, shaking his head as if Rook were the sorriest place he'd ever seen.

"Oh, this is nice," Henry said, grimly. "Wait'll you see Camp Nine."

The whistle blew again. I was so busy watching the boys marvel at the awfulness of my hometown that I didn't notice that Tom had gotten off the train and was standing in full dress uniform talking to a truck driver in the highway.

"So," said the Buddahead, "are there any dames there that aren't your sister?" The remark caused another round of catcalls and laughter, and somebody shoved him.

Tom shouted. "Fall in!"

Some of the boys bolted toward the trucks, and others shuffled behind like they weren't sure what they were supposed to do. Tom stood beside the first truck, directing the boys to climb inside the back. He gazed past me, a beguiling smile crossing his face.

Behind me, Mother stood off to the side of the highway. The hot wind from a passing truck caught her yellow-striped silk dress and sent it billowing around her lovely knees.

It was an old-fashioned dance in the Community Center, the kind they don't seem to have any more. A jukebox in the corner played Dick Haymes and Jo Stafford. Black-haired girls stood behind wooden tables and drew dripping Coca-Colas and beers from iced vats. Strictly forbidden by camp rules, Tom had managed to bring in alcohol just for this one event, and it was quickly disappearing. Children pilfered hot dogs from baskets and ran outside to enjoy them under the stars. Girls in party dresses bunched together in cliques around the periphery of the room, buzzing like swarms of hornets about which of the Hawaiians had populated their dance cards.

Mrs. Matsui sat off to the side, close enough to suggest, at first glance, that she was a part of the group. But as I looked closer, she seemed to have intentionally segregated herself from all the other people. Her sallow hands hung limp over her knees. Despite the gaiety, she was expressionless. Although her son, of whom she should have been rightfully proud, was home, she communicated with no one, but seemed lost to herself in the gay, undulating sea of people.

A miniature soldier with dark olive skin leaned against a square, whitewashed-wood column and nodded his head in time to the song. His name tag read "N. Fujita," and for the moment, he was the center of Mother's attention. "I was at university," he was saying, in an accent so thick I could barely understand his words. "The bombs hit and let me tell you, we were Johnny-on-the-spot. Reserve is what we were, but far as we were concerned, they needed us just the same."

Henry thrust a thumb at N. Fujita and grinned. "And then the army kicked Ned and his buddies out."

Ned shook his head. "Damn right." He clutched his hat to his chest and nodded at Mother. "Pardon my language, Miss."

Mother smiled, and I knew she'd heard worse. I'd heard her say worse, but Ned wouldn't have believed that. I listened in from a distance as he told his story. The first ones on the scene at Pearl Harbor, the Japanese American soldiers of Hawaii witnessed the brunt of the attack, an attack that was against them as much as anybody else.

"So, we all show up to guard the base. We got our rifles. Let me tell you, Miss, if we wanted to do anything bad, we had our chance. We had army-issue rifles, goddamn it!" He nodded respectfully again, as if begging a pass for his impolite choice of words. "Then, bam! They took away our commissions. Just like that. They didn't tell us anything, not even, 'Kiss my foot.'"

The Nisei, the first generation of American-born Japanese, were forbidden to defend their homeland. But they fought anyway—just to regain their rights to serve. Finally, the army decided it needed them, but it didn't realize that there was a difference between the Hawaiians and Californians. They put them all in the same unit, but it would take the shared struggles of Camp Nine to make them the cohesive force they would soon become.

Henry stood, and the cut of his pants fell just so. His hair was so short I could see his skin through it. His lean frame was visible beneath his clothes, his arms, thick and powerful.

"Chess."

It was David again. "You look real pretty today."

I smoothed my hands over the sheer fabric of my dress, then twisted my fingers together. "Thanks," I said.

"How old are you?"

"Thirteen."

He peered at me closely. "Don't get a crush on my brother, okay?" he said finally.

I was alarmed that my feelings were so easily read. What if Henry knew, too? "Hush up," I said. "Stop picking on me."

"I'm serious," he said. "He's too old for you."

Of course Henry was too old for me. I knew that much myself. But I was stinging from the embarrassment of having those feelings I couldn't control. "It's better than you and Audrey," I said.

I regretted immediately saying something both childish and nonsensical, but he seemed to take no offense. The side of his face lifted and curled into a charming grin. "You're pretty sharp for a kid," he said. "How did you know?"

His compliment pleased me, and I forgave him for noticing my attention to Henry. "I can just tell," I said, assuming an air of sophistication I didn't deserve. "Are you in love?" Since my experience in those matters was so limited, it was the only thing I could think to say.

"I don't know," he said brightly, as if it had never occurred to him to wonder. "She's a swell gal."

And then he abruptly wandered away.

Ned leaned in close to Mother. "These guys was crazy," he said, gesturing toward Henry. "Every week, they got their pay, and they didn't spend it or anything. Me and my guys, we're buying smokes and presents and blowing whole wads of cash on dillies, excuse me, miss, I mean girls. But you know what I mean."

Mother nodded.

Ned took a noisy swig from a bottle of beer. "Lots of fistfights." He moved his head in a broad circle. "What a bunch of dopes," he said. He thrust the bottle toward Henry. "We didn't have any idea. They were sending it home. Here," he said, swinging the bottle wildly in the air, the effects of the several beers he'd consumed becoming obvious.

He swallowed hard. "We didn't even know what they'd done to Henry's dad." He assumed a menacing stance. "Let me tell you, when I saw question twenty-eight, and saw that they took away Henry's dad and Henry was still gonna fight . . ."

Mrs. Matsui sat up straight as if a bullet had found her. A red tinge spread rapidly across her cheeks before she bolted from her chair. She'd made her exit so skillfully, however, that it seemed Henry and I were the only ones who noticed. Henry's eyes darted fleetingly after her, but he returned his attention to Ned, who tapped the bottle against his forehead to punctuate his closing comment. "No earthly idea."

Henry hopped from the stool and placed his arm around Ned's slight shoulder. Ned's head bobbed up and down, and his throat issued gurgling sounds as Henry steered him away from the group. Shortly before they reached me, Henry released him, and Ned veered off through a side door.

For the briefest of moments, Henry's eyes met mine. I didn't know whether he was thinking of his mother's sudden disappearance, or, like I was, that he would be leaving in the morning, this time for good. The boys would return to Camp Shelby, but it would be only days before they left for the front. He hesitated, then wove his way through his tipsy comrades toward me.

"Sorry about that," he said.

"About what?"

He shrugged his shoulders and cocked his head in the direction of the now-departed Ned Fujita.

The subject of Mr. Matsui's whereabouts sent Mother into such a rage, I never wanted to question her about it, although she'd tried to explain it calmly. Her details of the complicated issues just left me lost. David simply refused to discuss it. But Henry was different. I could talk to him. "Where is your dad?" I asked.

He shifted his weight. "He's in a prison camp in California called Tule Lake."

"What for?"

His explanation was a bit confusing at first. He called the questions the "Loyalty Oath," and finally told me what they were. "One asked if you would be willing to serve in combat duty," he said. "That was twenty-seven." He shrugged. "That one was okay. But question twenty-eight asked if you would faithfully defend the United States from all foreign and domestic attacks."

"What's wrong with that?"

"That wasn't all. It went on to ask you to renounce your allegiance to the emperor of Japan. It's a trick question, Chess."

"How could that be a trick question?"

He drew his mouth tight. "First of all, it begs the question," he said, his voice rising. "It assumes that you have allegiance to the emperor, which is just stupid. I've never even been to Japan. So if you said 'yes' to that, it implies that, at one time or another, you had some allegiance to the emperor. But also, my mother and father are Issei. That's what we call my parents' generation, the ones who were born in Japan. They can't become US citizens anyway. If they were to be deported to Japan, they might not be taken in there either. They'd be lost between two countries."

I waited for him to go on, but he paused.

"Did your dad say 'no' to the question?"

"He was too old to serve in the military, so he answered 'no' to twenty-seven. As for twenty-eight, well, he answered 'no' on principle. No and no. The men who answered 'no' to both questions are called no-no boys. And they sent all the no-no boys to Tule Lake. They're going to deport them to Japan."

I couldn't tell whether what he felt was sorrow or anger, but his words were clipped and troubled.

"Is that why your mother was so mad when Ned mentioned him?"

"She wasn't mad. She was ashamed. It's hard to explain to someone who's not Japanese. It's called *haji*: The idea that you mustn't bring shame to the family. Father being a no-no boy has brought dishonor to our family."

"I don't think so."

"That's because you're an American. Americans are more independent."

It would take many years and miles of travel before I understood what he meant. Henry told me that one of the defining things he loved about this country was that in America, a man was responsible only for his own choices. But in the Japanese culture of Henry's family, family honor was the most important thing. To the Issei, it was honorable to do what they were told by the authorities. Having to answer questions that didn't necessarily apply to them, or make sense under the circumstances, put the older generation in a terrible bind. Some people, like his father, intentionally rebelled, and for others, it was an honest misunderstanding. They really didn't understand the question.

"What did you say?"

"About what?"

"What did you say to question twenty-eight?"

His granite face relaxed. "I'm an American, Chess. I want to fight like everybody else. This is the only place I've ever lived, and I want to stay here. I answered 'yes.' To both."

"So, you're a yes-yes boy," I said.

"Yeah," he said. "I'm a yes-yes boy."

The tag on his chest spelled MATSUI and the idea that he was going away to fight brought me a sudden chill.

"Are you afraid?" I asked.

"No," he said, and, for some reason, I believed him. His skin was light olive and his hair was black. His brown eyes were slanted at the corners like Mother's were when she was angry. But he looked like an American soldier to me and I wasn't afraid either.

"Write to me," I said, the words fleeing my mouth before I had the chance to stop them.

To my surprise, he didn't laugh. He put his arm around me and pressed me against his starched shirt, and I inhaled its faint dampness. "I will write to you, Chess." He kissed my cheek, and I wanted my life frozen in that moment forever.

Chapter 12

Grandpa's cotton sat in the Morton Plantation trucks at the entrance to the cotton gin, waiting their turn to have their heavenly white loads weighed and processed. His trucks had already hauled in the last of Mother's crops, a special arrangement they enjoyed where he provided services to her farm, and she, in turn, paid him at least as much for the privilege as she would have paid a stranger. He would give no favors to a family member, nor would she have accepted any from him, so their arm's-length transactions suited them both just fine.

I followed Mother as she carefully picked her way toward the gin office, over and around muddy puddles in her high-heeled shoes, clutching her pocketbook among the buttons of her swing coat. "Is our cotton all in?" I asked.

"It certainly is," she said, dodging a pothole. "The beans, too. It's all in. The boys from Camp Nine were a godsend. We'd have never made it without them." She gave wide berth to the mule wagon of a tenant farmer. "But I'm glad it's over. They've got to get back to their studies."

As a Morton Plantation truck rolled past, the driver waved to Mother, and she returned it. I've since come to understand why Mother had her own place, separate from the Morton Plantation. It was a matter of independence. When Daddy died, she was left with only the proceeds of his life insurance policy—what had once been her source of income had disappeared into a puzzling, iron-fisted trust account in my name in McHenry. Daddy's share of the Morton Plantation had passed directly to me, his only heir. Grandpa's hand in that had been evident to Mother. It was his way of continuing control. But Mother did him one better. She made it despite him.

Although I was her natural child, not even Mother's guardianship of me was assured after Daddy's death. It was just business, Grandpa claimed, when he exerted his influence to have himself named my guardian instead of Mother. That such a thing could have happened in my lifetime is still shocking to me, and I can only imagine how she felt. She never voiced her frustrations about it to me, but I realize she could have picked up and left with me then, gone to another state, and fought him. But she understood that my place was on the plantation, whatever it might mean to her personal freedom. I wish I'd understood then all of the choices she made to preserve my interests over her own.

We walked inside the dingy office where Mr. Dewey Holt, the gin manager, sat behind a cluttered desk, his sleeves gathered into garters. As the bells on the glass tinkled, he looked up and smiled brightly. "Afternoon, Carrie!" Mother had that effect on men. Just her entrance into a room guaranteed the brightest part of their day. It was a gift at which I would always marvel, but never possess.

Mother removed one glove, then the other. "Hello, Dewey. I came to get my check."

Dewey scooted back his chair and rose. "Yes, ma'am. Got it in the safe. I'll only be a minute." He opened the latch on a gate and disappeared through a door.

Mother gestured toward a worn, wooden chair. "You may as well sit, Chess."

There was nothing interesting to see in the plain room. A cotton seed company calendar was still stuck on September. A freight train time-and-rate schedule presented a dizzying jumble of information I didn't understand. Dust gathered around the corners of a painting of ducks landing in a cypress slough.

Mother paced along the wooden railing separating the front of the room from the back. The stove in the corner cranked out copious amounts of heat and drew an odor of mildew from the walls. I took off my coat and laid it across my lap.

The sounds of the activity outdoors flooded the room as the door opened. Mother frowned. Upon seeing her, Mr. Ryfle frowned as well, but recovered quickly and touched his blackened fingers to the tip of his cap. "Miz Morton," he said.

She held her pocketbook closer. "Good afternoon, Hammond."

He removed his hat altogether and wiped his forehead with the back of his hand. Red scratches crisscrossed his cheek. "Lord a'mighty, can Dewey get it any hotter in here?" he brayed.

Mother forced the corners of her mouth up and fanned her face with her hand. "It is a bit warm."

He stamped the mud from his boots on the tile floor, the lumps of buckshot scattering under the chair rails. "Where is the old coot?"

"Gone in the back," she said.

He nodded.

A railway clock on the wall ticked, marking the uneasiness of the encounter.

"How's the family?" Mother said at length.

He protruded his lower lip. "Fine. Fine."

"The missus?"

"She's good. Knees are giving her fits, carrying that little one around. I told her make that child walk, but he cries up to high heaven she puts him down. Otherwise, can't complain."

"Well, that's to be expected."

"I suppose."

"How's Audrey enjoying her job?"

He set his jaw, then looked away. "I don't know it's doing her much good being around them people."

The muscles of Mother's face contracted. "How so?"

He moved the chaw of tobacco in his mouth to the other cheek and squinted at the ceiling tiles. "She's getting some funny ideals."

Dewey emerged from the back and passed through the wooden gate. "Howdy, Hammond," he said.

"Howdy."

"I'll be with you in a minute."

"Take your time."

Mother pursed her lips as Dewey selected an envelope from a slot on his desk and slid her check inside. He licked the edges and pressed down, then handed it to her. "Here you are, Carrie. Mighty good year you had. Better than most."

She slipped the envelope in her pocketbook, and its latch closed with a click. "Thank you, Dewey. I was blessed. Come on, Chess." I rose as she headed for the door.

Mr. Ryfle leaned toward the corner and shot a brown stream into a spittoon. "Miz Morton?"

Mother paused at the door. "Yes, Mr. Ryfle?"

He wiped at his mouth with a spotted handkerchief. "You probably don't want to hear this from me, but there's some folks not too happy 'bout them Japs being out there taking good jobs from decent folk."

"That's interesting to learn," she said. "Recall, Mr. Ryfle, that the reason I employed them was that you were shorthanded. Would you have had me let the field lie fallow?"

He stuffed the handkerchief back in his pocket.

"And, I would remind you," she continued, "that your personal feelings aside, your family enjoys the benefit of a steady income from Audrey's job."

"I'm just saying, is all. Thought you'd like to know."

She raised her chin. "I'm a widow who needs to earn a living. The opinions of others do not concern me."

"No'm. I don't guess they do," he said just as we were clearing earshot.

I'll never know, but will always suspect, that our encounter with Mr. Ryfle in some way contributed to Audrey's abrupt departure from her position at Camp Nine. Mother's remark about Audrey's steady job probably called into question Mr. Ryfle's status as the girl's father. And he couldn't have been any too pleased by Dewey Holt's comment to Mother that her farm had fared better than most that season, a direct affront to Mr. Ryfle's skills as a farmer.

While the Morton Plantation had been forced to cut back some on cultivation, all of the land that Mother had in crops had been expertly farmed by Homer, Cecil, and David and his friends, under the direction of Mr. Hayashida. Their yields were higher than had ever been achieved there, and now that the hundred acres were cleared, Mr. Hayashida had convinced Mother to grow a novel grain which would, over the years, prove to be her most profitable crop: rice. He'd leveled the ground and built a sophisticated irrigation system to flood the fields with the unlimited waters of Black Bayou.

And, whether it was intended to taunt Mr. Ryfle or just his nature as a born rebel, David had taken to flaunting his relationship with Audrey, and he became bolder about being seen in her company at Camp Nine. He could often be found hanging around outside the superintendent's office, and after Audrey's duties there were over for the day, he usually disappeared for an hour or two around the same time she went home. Now that Audrey was no longer there, he had settled into a dark mood.

One afternoon, I found him whiling away his time playing his guitar outside Mother's art classroom. I'd not heard him play since the day I followed him to Willie's, and his progress over these last several months was astounding. He'd mastered the signature style I had heard only that single time, but which was so remarkable, the memory of it would stay with me for life. Willie's blues style was to play both the melody and the rhythm with both hands, to form a sound so whole, no other instruments were needed. But more importantly, in Willie's style, the guitar itself, just six simple strings, actually sang the blues, as if it were speaking the words themselves. And they were words of rich African dialect.

Compelled to watch David's accomplishments, I left the

classroom and wandered close to where he sat beneath a window. He'd either made many, many more trips to Willie's, or he'd devoted countless days and nights to practice. It was probably a bit of both.

When he saw that he had a rapt audience, he gradually allowed the song to peter out, finishing it off with some aggressive fretwork and a pinched cry of the uppermost string.

I had never confronted him about his visits to Willie, but it seemed like a good time. I settled into the grass and waited for the last note to die down. "You've been sneaking out."

His face became blank, as if he were weighing whether or not denying it was worth the effort. His heavy lids blinked slowly. "So what?" he said.

"You could get caught."

He paused, then smiled broadly and reached in his pocket. He flashed a beige slip of cardboard. "Not any more. I have a pass."

"You don't understand. You could get in trouble just talking to Willie. People around here don't allow it."

He stuffed the pass back in his pocket and took issue with my warning, reminding me that his meeting Willie was my idea in the first place. I couldn't believe he would twist my innocent comment against me, however rash it had been.

He smiled again, a relaxed, confident grin that almost convinced me he was right. "Don't worry, Chess. Nobody knows. Not unless you tell them. It's kind of your own doing, isn't it?"

I remembered what Ruby Jean had said about the Japanese being safe if they stayed on their own side of the fence. Maybe it had been Mother's fault for bringing them outside to work, but David was deliberately making things worse.

"I just wish you'd stay home," I said. "It's not just you. Willie could get in trouble, too."

He began a simple, gentle strumming. "You worry too much."

But then it dawned on me that there was more to his wanderings than visits to Willie. "You're seeing Audrey out of camp, aren't you?"

He pretended to concentrate on the strings. "I'm just picking up information here and there, that's all." Audrey had been speaking freely to him about Mr. Ryfle's activities to rebuild the Klan.

"Mother says Mr. Ryfle's just a silly old fool," I said. "It's not going to amount to anything."

His hand slammed flat against the sound box. "Chess, it's the principle of the thing. We're all locked up in this camp while that jackass is free to run loose and do anything he wants."

I was at a loss for words as his fingers twiddled teasingly over some high notes. Why did I even care about what happened to David? He seemed intent on his own destruction.

"He's evil," he said. "He's hurt Audrey. And he's going to keep hurting her until somebody stops him."

I knew he was right, at least about that part. I had already suspected it. First, when Audrey had failed to appear for her job at Camp Nine, Miss Lilly had called Mother, thinking she might know where Audrey was. When Audrey didn't show up three days in a row, Mother paid a visit to the Ryfles' home and was met on the porch by Mrs. Ryfle, who informed her that Audrey would no longer be working at Camp Nine.

But what I saw myself occurred the day that Cecil drove up to Grandma's house with a deer he'd shot. Grandpa met him in the yard and, after admiring "the old gentleman," as Cecil called him, told him to dress the animal in the barn out back.

As Cecil piloted the truck through a blanket of goldenrod, Mr. Ryfle's prehistoric Dodge pickup truck wheezed around the corner and coasted to a stop under the mulberry tree. Four little Ryfle children ranged around the bed, craning their necks over the edge to look around.

Audrey sat in the front seat, but she gazed away in the other direction through the window, as Mr. Ryfle opened the driver's side and alighted. He raked his hat from his head. "I thank you kindly letting me know about the deer meat, Mr. Morton."

"Those kids got to eat, Hammond."

"Yessir."

"Cecil's already taken him on back to the barn to dress him. You can meet up with him back there and take your pick. But mind you, Cecil gets the backstrap and Mrs. Morton needs a few pounds of sausage. I've told Cecil that you can have the rest."

Mr. Ryfle flopped his hat back onto the top of his head and wrenched it down tight around his ears. "Much obliged, Mr. Morton."

I walked in a circle around to the front of the truck, but wherever I stood, Audrey managed to avoid me.

The rusty truck creaked as Mr. Ryfle scaled the running board and thrust his head in the cab. He scowled at Audrey and she flinched. "Tell the people thank you, Miss High-and-Mighty," he said.

She twisted her head downward and mumbled.

"Say it so they can hear it!" he bellowed.

She paused, then turned her face to me. The entire side was a palette of purples and yellows, where a black eye on the mend had spread. Her eyes met mine, and she held them there. "Thank you, Chess," she said quietly.

I'd felt as if I might faint as the truck squeaked on its springs and bumped down the dirt road away from me.

As justified and invincible as he might have felt, David was no match for someone of such a volatile nature. "You can't do anything to stop Mr. Ryfle," I said. "You're just a kid."

"I won't be alone," he said.

As Mother approached in the distance, I knew the conversation was ending. "What does that mean?"

He watched over my shoulder as she drew nearer. I leaned in close to him. "Who?" I hissed.

His expression was maddening, and he was doing it on purpose. I wanted to throttle him, but he just acted as though nothing was happening, twirled the pick between his fingers, and struck a merry tune.

Chapter 13

Henry kept his promise and wrote to me often. Sometimes the letters came all at once, bundled in rubber bands, and then weeks might pass without a single note. But each one brought me the sound of his voice as surely as if he were sitting with me. A great deal of what he said, though, was lost to the censors' random judgments, and his letters were invariably crossed through in critical areas with black lines. I understood that the letters weren't supposed to give us any information about troop movements, but how could I travel along with Henry if I didn't know where he was?

"Missing you and Miss Carrie and everybody at Camp Nine," the latest letter read. "Bet it's cold as heck there, isn't it?"

Ordinarily, his prediction would have been right, but our December was unusually warm, almost like March all over again. Slender, green grasses shot up in the wet ditches, and pink buds peeked from the tip of the lone tulip tree in our yard.

Mother laughed at his latest one. The censors had let slip two crucial details—he said that all the women looked like Mother. And he signed off with "ciao."

"He wants us to know he's in Italy," she said.

I was thrilled that he was sending me clues. My mind drifted to the box of yellowed postcards Mother had from relatives in Italy addressed to her own mother. Although they were black and white, their pictures of villages set on high cliffs and boats moored in cozy ports had always fueled my imagination. All the way to Camp Nine, as I sat in the front seat of the car with a plate of warm pastries in my lap, I pictured him sitting atop a blue mountain, thinking of small delights he might slip into his letters just to please me.

"I'm glad he's somewhere pretty," I said as Mother made the turn down a dirt lane toward the back of the camp. "Maybe they're not fighting in Italy."

She stopped the Buick in the mud next to a row of barracks and frowned. "They're fighting plenty hard there," she said grimly.

We opened both our doors at the same time and a warm wind filled the car with a false promise of spring. Mother stepped lightly down the wooden planks that bobbed and sucked in the buckshot. Behind her, I carried a cloth-covered plate of apricot fried pies tucked up under my arm.

"I hate coming unannounced," she said, her gloved hands poised to knock on the door of the barracks.

I clutched the pies, as nervous as she was. "Henry made us promise."

"I know," she said, sighing and knocking lightly on the plain door.

Mrs. Matsui opened the door, but her appearance took me aback. She looked so unlike herself it took me a moment to recognize her. Instead of her brilliant wrapped silks, she was shapeless in a pastel-colored housedress, and her feet were tucked into tiny, wooden slippers. She wore no makeup, and her hair appeared not to have been washed in days. It had been bound up against the top of her head in a scarf, but who could tell how long ago that had been? It sprang loosely from all sides.

She pressed her hands to her head and fidgeted with the scarf. "Carrie," she said softly. "Oh, my, and Chess, too. Oh, dear." She backed away from the door.

"I'm sorry for just dropping in," Mother said. "Ruby Jean and I made some pies, and Chess and I thought we would just surprise you with a couple."

But it was a lie.

Henry's last letter had alarmed her. "Can you ask your mom to please check on Mother?" it had said. "She never writes to me. David says she's fine, but I can't be sure he isn't just saying that so that I won't be concerned."

Mother didn't even ask Ruby Jean for any help. Or me, either, for that matter. She'd flown into the kitchen like a mad woman and whipped up several batches of fried pies as a prop, an excuse to make her visit. I was then holding them under my arm on a heavy plate while Mrs. Matsui stood in the door, unmoving, looking away as if she would rather we were not there.

"Sakura?" Mother said after a moment. "Can we come in?"

Mrs. Matsui stared at her feet and nodded. "Yes. Yes, please come in."

Mother took the steps up into the barracks, and held the door for me. I carried the pies inside and searched for a free space to place them. I didn't consider myself a neat person, but even I could see that the room was a mess. Piles of clothes cluttered an unmade bed. An overheated woodstove glowed in the corner. Stacked papers threatened to topple over of their own accord.

Mrs. Matsui sank rigidly into a simple chair. Without another word, Mother opened the woodstove and picked away at it with a poker. When she raised the window, a cool breeze refreshed the room.

Everything there, including Mrs. Matsui, seemed to be decomposing, and I was embarrassed to be in the middle of it. Anxious to retreat into something, I picked up one of David's schoolbooks and pretended to concentrate on chapter 16, "Electromagnetism and Your World." Mother flung aside the stale bedclothes to air, then opened a wardrobe and began hanging rumpled shirts and pants on hangers.

Tiny sounds came from Mrs. Matsui and her pale, knobby knees began to tremble. Mother held her head firmly straightforward and inspected a dress for wrinkles. "What's going on, Sakura?" she asked gently.

Mrs. Matsui dabbed at her eye with the hem of her housedress and rocked back and forth in her seat.

"Chess," Mother said, "go outside and see if Edo's growing anything in the garden."

I was grateful for the escape. I placed the book on the table, instead of the floor where I had found it, and slipped out the door and down the steps.

I followed a trail of planks toward the very back edge of the camp, winding my way between the barracks, their windows open to take advantage of the unseasonable warmth. Lively voices issued from inside, children giggling, adults squabbling. But I wasn't paying them attention. My mind was on Henry sitting on his imaginary mountaintop in Italy. For once, I was glad that he wasn't at Camp Nine.

The path ended at the edge of a broad field where Mr. Hayashida's dormant garden spread in tan rows like stripes on corduroy toward the graying woods. The sun blazed in the clear, bright sky. Songbirds twittered and chirped out of season and the green grass along the edge of the field glittered.

I heard shouts in the distance, boys caught up in a spirited game of football. I wondered if David was in the game, playing while his mother came apart at the seams back in their lonely apartment.

In a far corner, Mr. Hayashida worked a hoe in a bucket. He spotted me and waved.

My feet sank into the soft dirt as I made my way toward him.

"You want to help me, Chess?" he asked.

"Yessir," I said, brushing the hair from my eyes.

"Where is your mother?"

"With Mrs. Matsui."

He stood over a bucket, gripping the handle of the hoe in his wrinkled glove. He nodded. "Carrie will be good for her."

"What's happening to her?"

He pulled the hoe from the bucket and dropped it in the grass. "Sakura's having bad problems," he said. "The other women at Camp Nine have shunned her."

I stepped into the middle of a frame of two-by-fours which he'd nailed together in a rectangle and set into the ground. "Why would they do that?"

He lifted a bag, straining his face into furrows. "You have to understand, Chess," he said, pouring sand into the bucket. "We are a people of close families." Coming to Camp Nine was devastating to the families, he explained, breaking them up. Children didn't sit with their parents at meals. They no longer followed the strict traditions that promoted respect for their elders. Sons were off at war, fighting and dying. Daughters were leaving to clean distant hotels. Fathers who stood up for what they believed were sent to prison. Nothing was the same for these people as it had been.

A warm breeze ruffled bare branches above our heads. They whistled as the air moved through their sharp tips. "But it wasn't her fault," I said.

He twisted the cap of a garden hose and squirted water into the bucket. "It's human nature," he said. "When people are afraid, they want to blame somebody, even if it doesn't make any sense." But there was more, he told me. Because David worked for Mother, his pass out of camp allowed him to run out all hours of the day and night. The other mothers believed that he showed Sakura disrespect, and that she, in return, was weak to allow him to behave that way.

He twisted the cap closed to cut off the spray. "And their husbands are not at Tule Lake. Two men from the army were here last week. They had an assembly for us, served cake and punch, showed us a movie. It was all a lot of fun. They wanted to reward Camp Nine for having the fewest disloyals. See, that's very big to the Japanese. We go out of our way to play by the rules all the time. If one of us doesn't, it makes us all look bad."

He stirred the contents of the bucket with the blade of the hoe. "Help me, will you?" He pointed to the ground. "Hold that frame still while I pour this concrete."

I stepped outside the frame, crouched on my ankles, and held the two-by-fours steady.

"Mr. Hayashida, do you think of yourself as Japanese or as American?"

He didn't answer me. He lifted the bucket, tilted it, and poured muddy gray concrete into the form. I watched it spread slowly to the four corners and fill the space, feeling that perhaps I'd somehow offended him with the question. "My other grandpa was from Italy. But then he became an American," I explained.

"I'm an American," he said, nodding briskly once. "But I was born in Japan."

The concrete reached the edges and stopped. We stood together and watched it as if we were waiting for it to do something else. He knelt. "Question twenty-eight was a terrible thing," he said, flicking off the bits of dust and debris that had floated down and settled on the face of the concrete. "It divided the community." He wiped his hands, straightened, and lifted the now-empty bucket. He strode slowly and deliberately away from me, one foot in front of the other, heel to toe, as if measuring something of which he was already sure.

"It made enemies of friends. The other ladies flaunt their families to Mrs. Matsui. They don't mean to do it, but they do. Family is the most important thing to the Issei."

"Henry said that honor is the most important thing to the Issei," I said.

He stopped in front of another wooden frame, identical to the one we had just filled. "In our culture, they are the same."

"What did you say to question twenty-eight?" I asked.

He contemplated the ground, his lips drawn up tight, looking as if he might whistle had he not been so sad. After a moment, he smiled gamely. "I'm still here, aren't I?"

I've wondered over the years what he had thought when he'd answered 'yes' those two times. Had the answer been a struggle for him, or had he easily resigned to his knowledge that America guaranteed freedom to only a few?

"Well?" he said brightly. "Where's all my help?"

I jumped up and ran to him, settled to the ground, and held the frame steady in my hands.

"That's my girl," he said.

"My teachers say sometimes I annoy people with questions," I said, as the glop splashed into the frame like melted chocolate ice cream and spread outward in thick, rippled waves.

He tilted the side of the bucket until the last drop of wet concrete trickled into the rectangle. "The world would be a better place if the government stopped asking questions of the people, and the people started asking questions of the government," he said. "That's the way it should be in America."

He set the bucket on the ground and walked a few paces to a wooden rake lying in the tall, blowing grass. He leaned forward at the waist, his hand on the small of his back as if it pained him to bend so deeply, and lifted the rake by the handle.

It was not an ordinary rake. Instead of tines, the handle secured a board upon which were pieces of wood which had been cut into odd characters. Mr. Hayashida tested the first slab of concrete with the tip of his finger. He pushed the rake firmly into the soft concrete, leaning his weight into the handle. After a moment, he gently tapped it loose and lifted it.

Inside the wooden form, a long, gray slab had taken shape. Japanese characters trailed across the top.

"What does it say?" I asked.

He pressed a star-shaped stencil into the soft concrete underneath the lines of characters. "They are names," he said.

"Names?"

"Names of our boys," he said.

I looked around me, and noticed a small, low fence and a gravel walk, which were new to that part of the garden.

"What is this?"

He pulled the stencil from the concrete, leaving a perfect imprint of an army star in the gray slab. He tossed the star shape into the grass, placed his arm around my shoulder, and pulled me to his side, squeezing me gently with his crooked arm.

I knew the answer as it left his mouth.

"This is where we say goodbye to our sons."

Cherry blossoms are pink.

It is said that, thousands of years ago, the cherry blossom was white. One day during a terrible battle, the warriors of the emperor fought valiantly, but they were killed. To honor them, the emperor buried the bodies of all the fallen warriors beneath his prized cherry tree. The next morning, the emperor awoke to find that all of the blossoms of the tree had turned red from their spilled blood. To this day, the blossoms of the cherry tree are bright pink.

Here is another one: The samurai of Japan prized the cherry blossom because it was so beautiful, but it only lived a few days. A warrior on his way to battle was forbidden to cross a field covered with cherry blossoms because they were sacred. Legend says that the tree is like God, and each blossom that falls to the ground is the soul of a warrior who has sacrificed himself for his mission.

Mr. Hayashida promised that he would get me a cherry tree from California. He said it might not grow in Arkansas, but that we would have to try. He thought it might not arrive from Sacramento until as far away as May. But that would be good, he said. Because winter would be over then, and it might have a chance to live in that cold, unforgiving place.

Chapter 14

By early spring, Mother had begun to carry the constant vexed expression I recalled from our days before Tom came to us, and I knew that the end of their relationship was nearing. He was at Camp Nine less often, and on the rare occasions that he was there, I was excluded from their conversations.

Mother and I had never discussed Tom, other than with regard to the obvious: when he was coming to Camp Nine, when he would be returning to Mississippi, what he might like her to cook for supper. Since Daddy's death, and until Tom had arrived, there had never been any occasion to talk about any man, other than Grandpa, Mr. Ryfle, or one of the field hands. And if we talked about one of those men, it wasn't in the context of the fact that he *was* a man and what place he had in our lives. It would have been out of the question to have suddenly opened for discussion the nature of Tom's relationship with us and where it might lead. Besides, as it was evolving, I suppose I knew that if I questioned her, she would realize that I understood more than she thought I did, and that she might end their affair. That possibility was a chance I couldn't take, so desperate was I to have him there.

But it did seem cruel that their tension came to a head in spring, when the crocus had disappeared back into the ground and our yard was a riot of tulips and daffodils. We'd spent a brief afternoon at Tom's, both Mother and he hardly exchanging words. What conversation they did have was cursory and polite.

It had started to drizzle when Mother asked me to wait for her outside.

I bundled the collar of my rain slicker around my neck, thrust my hands in my pockets, and walked the wet perimeter of Tom's porch, trying to appear occupied with something, but listening as best I could. The zinnias she'd cultivated in his planter the summer before were nothing then but shriveled twigs. I snapped them in half to pass the time.

What followed was a terrible, and as far as I know, final, argument between them. Unknown to me, Mother had been quietly waging a campaign to have Mr. Matsui released from Tule Lake and returned to his family. Her single-mindedness toward this goal must have put a strain on their already fragile relationship.

She was so angry, her voice carried clearly through the thin glass panes. "You promised to try!"

"I personally delivered your letter to the war department," Tom said. "Do you have any idea what the reaction was to that?"

"I know it puts you in a bind," she said, "but you're the only person who can help."

There was a long pause, and I wandered closer to the window to catch the rest.

Tom spoke slowly, each word measured equally. "I've risked everything that means anything to me." There was another long pause. "For you," he added, at length.

I couldn't hear what she said in return, but his next words surprised us both. "I'm not supposed to tell this to anyone. But I'm going to tell you. They're closing Camp Nine."

Camp Nine was closing. As hard as I tried, I couldn't imagine life without it.

I could almost hear her smile. "Then they'll close Tule Lake, too."

"I won't have any reason to come back," he said. "Carrie?"

The floorboard creaked again. "I'm sorry, Tom," she said. "Thank you for all you've done."

And that was the end of it. I was disappointed and angry with her. I knew my mother well enough to know that she wasn't just using Tom for her personal agenda. She truly had loved him. I knew that. And yet, my childish self-interest kept me from understanding her. It seemed impossible to me that, after all that had happened, that after here, in DeSoto County, of all places, she had found him again, she would place what then seemed to me to be pointless meddling before her love for him and what could be a future for us as a family.

Of course, that wasn't the case at all. In the end, it was neither honor nor ambition that sealed the fate of that relationship. It was simple reality. I realize now that we could never have had Tom freely. Even if he had thought he was willing to give up everything for her, the truth was that he had obligations from which he would never be able to escape. It was an empty fantasy, and she had the presence of mind to understand that. But at the time, I could only try to reconcile the things I saw and the things I heard with the things I so very much wanted to be true.

I bolted from my spot and busied myself at the base of the steps. The screen door sprang shut and Mother took the steps quickly from the porch.

"Ready, Chess?" she said absently.

"Yes, ma'am."

"Well, let's get on home. Colonel Tom has to get on back to Mississippi."

As she slung her scarf over her head, the sudden wind caught the front of her scarf, and billowed it up and out like a parachute. With her left hand, she pulled it taut against her hair. With her right, she drew the corner to her face and raked it secretively across her eyes.

———

The next day, Mother closed the curtains with a clothespin and climbed into bed with a rag over her forehead. She didn't venture out of her room for days, except to wander weakly to the bathroom, tilting and weaving in pain, her hands groping along the wall to guide her there and then back again. Ruby Jean swore Mother had never before had a sick headache that had lasted that long. She became so worried, she got on the telephone and had the operator call Dr. Mason in McHenry. He made the eleven-mile trip to the house and gave Mother a shot of morphine that he said would knock her out all day. She slept soundly afterwards.

Every part of my life was changing. No longer content to climb trees and catch tadpoles from the drainage ditches, I had become as restless as I had ever seen my mother. While she lay sick in bed, I sat for an hour or two after dinner in Daddy's chair and leafed listlessly through a book of poetry, absorbing none of what I read. Mid-afternoon, Ruby Jean appeared in my door, dishtowel in hand, her voice barely a whisper. "Chess?"

"What?"

She looked over her shoulder down the hall. "Mr. Walter here. Say he want to talk to you."

"Grandpa?"

She nodded vigorously. I took my time, while she scurried into the kitchen. "She coming, Mr. Walter!" she chirped through the back door.

Grandpa stood in the backyard near the bird feeder, filling out his khaki-colored suit too well around the middle. His eyes squinted through round lenses at our roof as if he thought there was something wrong with it, and he fidgeted with the brim of his hat. The screen door escaped my grip and slammed, causing him to turn.

"I hear your Mama's down."

"Yessir."

He pushed his glasses up the bridge of his nose. "Well, that's too bad."

"Yessir."

I waited on the porch, wishing he would say something that would give me some idea of what he wanted. He puffed up with a full breath and stuck his thumbs in his suspenders, gazing around our yard without any apparent purpose.

He looked up at me as if I'd only just then appeared. "Let's you and me go for a ride," he said brightly.

I'd never been alone in the same room with my grandfather, much less been cooped up in a car with him. The seconds dragged as I took each step off the back porch one at a time, ducking my head so that he couldn't see the fluster rise in my face.

He waited for me, then fell in step beside me. "That be alright with you?" he asked, as if I were still a small child.

"Yessir."

He stopped abruptly in the middle of the path. "Then for heaven's sake, child, stand up straight! You're goddamn pretty, just like your mother. Let everybody see it."

I lifted my head and pulled my shoulders back, sticking my chin up higher. "That's better," he said, holding open the gate between our houses. "Come on. I want to show you something."

The Lincoln Continental glided like a battleship down Highway 1, the world outside slipping past us in a blur of images. Grandpa had one hand on the big steering wheel and the opposite arm draped out the window. "I got two grandchildren," he said. "Both girls. Both born right together. I used to think I was cursed that way, not having any boys to take over the place. But I got used to it a long time ago. All I got's two girls." He shook his head. "But Babe's no good."

I gave him a quick glance, but he just stared ahead, squinting and grinning.

"Flighty, just like her mother. That's why I'm leaving this place to you someday, Chess. I'm counting on you to keep it going when I'm gone, and I want to show it to you proper. Not just a Sunday drive, but show it to you for real. You got to get to know every inch of it. Where it came from and what it can do. Every acre is different."

The guard towers of Camp Nine loomed against the sky on the

other side of the tracks. Grandpa lifted his arm and thrust his thumb casually in their direction. "Camp Nine," he said. "That was your land. I know you know it 'cause your mama chewed my ass about it for a whole year. She's a good woman, Chess, and don't think I don't know it. But she's got a soft streak a mile long and out here it doesn't do you any good. Fifty years ago, this land wasn't anything but cane-brake and bottomland. Now there's opportunity as far as the eye can see. If you stop to think about what's fair, the Delta will pass you flat by, girl. Do you hear me?"

A man with a rifle paced in the tower nearest us.

"Yessir."

"That's my girl," he said as the towers faded in the rearview mirror. "I was having so much fun with your mama, I couldn't stand to put her out of her misery. I didn't steal nothing from you. Your money's in a trust in the bank in McHenry. I got it in gov'ment bonds. When this war is over, the price of that land'll hit rock bottom and I'll buy it back for you for next to nothing."

We veered off Highway 1 onto the main dirt road that led through the place. Almost the entirety of the Morton Plantation lay on either side of that winding, rutted road. The Lincoln bounced and jostled over the holes, and shook and shimmied along the ridged edges.

"I know your grandma doesn't favor you much," Grandpa said as the car slid a bit sideways in the thick gravel. "She's a difficult woman." He shook his head. "She could start an argument in an empty house. 'Course, she was raised rich and never had to do a lick of work in her whole life. And that's where I got to hand it to your mama. She never raised you like a rich girl."

On either side of us, fields lay to the forests on the far horizon. The broad, flat leaves of shoulder-high plants baked in the sun, dizzying waves of heat shimmering up into the sky.

I couldn't find my tongue.

"I guess you don't recollect your daddy too much, do you, girl?"

I remembered everything about him. I remembered his clothes

and his work boots. I remembered his shirts hanging by the back door and his truck and his long, slender fingers and his Stetson hat. I remembered the wrinkles around his eyes when he smiled.

"No, sir," I said, because it was less complicated than the truth.

The Lincoln rattled over a cattle guard and climbed straight up into the sky, evening out onto the flat, gravel road that ran atop the levee. "That boy was the best hunter I ever saw," Grandpa said. "He loved you and your mama. Loved you both till the day he died. And he loved this land."

The Lincoln lurched suddenly down a small path, straight down the side of the levee. My stomach fell out from under me, and I gripped the door of the car until we came to a stop at the remnants of an abandoned village. In front of us, stretching away from the levee, a quiet slough wound among banks of cypress trees hooded with Spanish moss. Grandpa turned the key and the engine fell silent. In the hushed afternoon, I felt as though I could hear the vines growing among the fallen-down shacks.

Grandpa opened his door and got out, so I did the same. He sauntered along a ridge to the edge of the slough. "Your mama ever bring you out here?" he asked.

I walked with great care through the weeds, certain that we were greatly outnumbered by snakes. "No, sir."

He stood on a mud bank overlooking the water. "No, I don't expect she would. Maybe she didn't know."

I clambered up on top of a cypress knee several yards away, my fingers clutching the wispy, frayed bark of a sapling.

He gazed out to the other side. "This was your daddy's favorite spot. He'd come out here with a fishing pole and haul in gar that were fifteen feet long if they were an inch." He picked up a stone from the ground and skittered it across the one swath of water that was not overgrown with brilliant green plants. An army of turtles of various sizes slid into the emerald soup. On the other side, an ebony water moccasin wove a ribbon toward a dilapidated clapboard shack with a fallen-in roof. Spindly trees grew out of and in between the walls.

"Who lives here?" I asked.

He pulled a handkerchief from his breast pocket, took off his glasses, and wiped the sweat from his eyes. "Lord, child, no one's lived here in forty years. This isn't nothing but the old levee camp."

A sudden breeze lifted its voice and sang through the boards and the trees and the fallen porches. "Grandpa."

He turned.

"Tell me about the levee camps."

He squinted at me as if he were looking directly into the sun. The wind picked up, rustling the fabric of my shirt, kicking up the dry grass at our feet, and whispering through a broken pane of glass.

"They were terrible places, honey. Wasn't any law in them at all." His eyes were fixed behind the twin round wire frames. He said nothing for a moment, then hitched up his trousers and took large, bold steps toward me. He waved a hand toward a fallen tree, beckoning me to sit. And I did.

His squint softened and he settled down next to me. He flicked the brim of his hat with an index finger, his pale eyes taking in the whole of our surroundings. "Back in those days," he said "you could make more money building levee any day than you could hoping a heavy rain doesn't come and wash your crop away. Your great-grandpa held the contract to build this piece of the levee and most of his hands worked out here. Right about the time your daddy was born, Old Mr. Heston died, and I had to take the place over."

The handkerchief went once over his face again. "All I can tell you, girl, is that I tried to do the right thing. We had troubles that you couldn't imagine. How people end up living like that, I don't know. Old Charlie Ryfle, that was Hammond's daddy, was the worst of the bunch."

"You knew Mr. Ryfle's father?"

He chuckled. "Knew him?" He took off his hat and ran the palm of his hand over the top of his bald head. "Yeah, I knew him. 'Mister Cholly,' the hands used to call him. He was known up and down the Delta as the meanest foreman on the Arkansas side. There's a special place in hell for people like Charlie. I expect he's still there."

This conversation was something new to me, something so entirely different. I'd spent the whole of my life being afraid of my grandparents, cold and imperious as they were. As much as I had dreaded this encounter, my grandfather was offering me something no one else ever had: a sense of my place in the mystery of the Delta.

"Grandpa?" I ventured timidly.

He looked at me kindly.

"Why are the levee people so different?" I asked.

"They are different," he said, "but they're fine folks." He nodded agreeably. "They may not be educated or have fancy things, but they're good people. They have a different way of living than you and I do. But that's only because we're the haves and they're the have-nots. And frankly, girl, the things we have they don't really need."

He pointed toward the levee. "I know men living in houseboats on the river with ten kids and a fat wife who're nothing but content, long as they can work odd jobs and fish in the afternoon."

He frowned deeply. "It's nothing wrong with most levee folks. But Charlie Ryfle . . ." He paused and placed his hat back on his head. "The whole lot of the Ryfles is rotten to the core."

If I ever had a chance to learn the truth, it was now. "Grandpa?"

"What, girl?"

"What is the bad blood between the Mortons and the Ryfles?"

He folded the handkerchief into a triangle. He unfolded it and folded it back again, then thrust it in his pocket and looked away. "Why, honey," he said at length, "there's no such thing."

So that was it. The bad blood didn't even exist. It was only a figment of Ruby Jean's imagination, something to knock me off course and stop me from asking her questions. I should have known it was a myth, otherwise, I'd have heard the story passed among the townsfolk like rolls at a dinner table. By now, Ruby Jean would have forgotten she'd even said those things. I would just have to let go of the notion altogether.

He stood. "Come on. We got miles to go. You got a lot to learn today. And your mama's going to want you home for supper."

We walked away as the levee camp shimmered behind us on the banks of the emerald slough like a mirage. The doors of the Lincoln closed behind us, heavy steel slamming shut like the deep secret vault of a bank.

"Mr. Gilwell say you got something COD in the mail," Ruby Jean said, hanging up the phone. "Say it some kind of knobby plant or something."

It had been months.

I took a final swig of my Coke and slammed my napkin on the table. "Thank you for lunch, Ruby Jean," I said, bolting down the hallway. She mumbled something about my manners behind me, loud enough so that I could hear, but not loud enough that I would know that she meant for me to.

I fell to my knees before my bottom drawer, pulled out the treasure box, and dumped its contents onto the oval braided rug on my floor. How long had it been since I'd even opened it, other than to stuff Henry's letters inside for safekeeping? The shells and the arrowheads, the feather, the spool of purple thread, the fossilized nautilus, and Henry's letters all went back into the cedar box. I stowed the Spanish coins and the gold cross in my pocket and lit out for Mr. Gilwell's store. Mother had been right. The day had come and finally there was something that was more important. The cherry tree had arrived from California.

I considered it a special event that afternoon, as I sat in the grass while Cecil dug a deep hole in the rich Delta earth, gently placed the root ball inside, and together, we carefully replaced the topsoil around the tender trunk. That evening, I sat in the window of my bedroom as the light faded, and watched the tree's small branches soak up the last of the daylight until darkness overtook us both.

Chapter 15

As in any other town in America, baseball was all the rage that summer at Camp Nine. Most of the boys played from the minute they rose until it was time to go to bed. Modern electric lights allowed play at all hours.

Things were vastly different at the Kimble School, where the meager field was poor and dirty. Devoid of grass, home plate was nothing more than a burlap bag filled with corn. But improvements would have been lost on the levee boys. Since their summers were filled with back-breaking labor, they did not have the luxury of being religious in their zeal toward any sport. In their world, there were no major league baseball teams to root for, and no electricity for radio broadcasts of the teams from Brooklyn or Chicago playing the World Series. Their skill at baseball consisted of getting out on the field with a ball and a bat, and swinging as hard as they could, hoping that somebody would get hurt. Now, that was entertainment.

Since the summer before, Mother had been organizing this league between the locals and the camp boys as a way for them to pass the summer constructively. She'd had only the best of intentions, thinking it might give the farm boys a recreational outlet, and give the Japanese boys somebody to play with aside from each other. But as we trudged through the dewy grass to the cracked and splintered bleachers, burdened by her secret knowledge that Camp Nine might be closing, she'd lost her enthusiasm for the idea, and I dreaded being back at my old school on a Saturday morning. "Why don't they just play at Camp Nine?" I asked, grumbling.

Mother's shoes were collecting stickers. "The locals are already mad enough that they have electricity at the camp," she said low. "No need to let them see what a nice field they have on top of everything else."

She hiked her cotton skirt at the knees and took the bleachers two at a time. I followed her, and we took our seats at the top. On the ground below us, dew sparkled like diamonds in the warming morning sun, and a meadowlark picked around for worms.

I took Henry's latest letter from my pocket to pass the time. I couldn't have cared less about the game.

"These battalions sit on the lines all winter, until we go and make the breakthrough," it said, "because they can't go anywhere until we do. Then they take off too fast, like they aren't even thinking and they get trapped again. I think that's the whole reason they send in the 442nd. They don't care if we get killed. They just want us there to get the other battalions out of harm's way. But then when we take a town, they don't even let us enjoy anything. We get all the way to the outskirts and make it safe, and then they call out 'Hold up!' We sit there in the mud while the 36th goes in on tanks and gets all the girls with the flowers in their hands."

I slipped the first page behind the second one.

"But, boy, I wish you could see some of the old buildings and things that I've seen. You would really love it, in peace time, that is. Statues and artwork and history all over the place."

"Batter up!"

Boys from the Kimble School were already sprinkled out in the field. They were a sad sight, small and scrawny, compared to their opponents. The Camp Nine boys were two to three years older than almost all of the Kimble kids. Some of the boys had brought their big brothers to play, but even they would not be as skilled as the Japanese boys. They were going to get creamed, and I was not too keen to see it happen.

The pitcher slammed the ball into his glove, then fished it out, and repeated it. Mr. Brown, serving as umpire, called out the game. Jesse Ryfle squirmed like a new puppy on third. The first batter, a Japanese boy of seventeen or eighteen, got a hit. The batter ran the bases and stopped at second. An outfielder lifted the ball from the ground and threw it to second base, but the runner was already safe.

Mother had been able to get the boys passes for the game, but Mr. Brown thought it was too risky for the parents to attend, so there was no support from the stands for the batter. Mother and I clapped for him, but the locals in the seats in front of us glared. Mother smiled at them, and they returned their sour faces to the game. Fortunately, it didn't appear that the game would last very long.

And I had Henry's letter to keep me company.

"Here's why we're so good," it said. "Up there in the forest, the enemy's ten or fifteen feet away. We fight with tommy guns, because it's such close quarters. But tommys use .45-caliber ammunition, which you can only get from tanks. So the tanks roll, and we walk right beside them. We knock on the outside, and the guy sticks his hand out the window and drops the bullets right out the window. It's the darndest thing I ever saw. The Germans are all hidden in the trees and the bushes. We're hidden, too, but we can see them better than they can see us because they're so pale, right? They can only stay hidden so long before they have to peek out to see what's happening, and then, pow! That's when we fire at them. It's kind of like a game, you know?"

I didn't know if he was serious or only trying to make me laugh, but a laugh was what he got. As I looked around the baseball field, though, I thought that maybe it was true. The levee boys were pale and white, except for their necks and ears, which were ruddy with sunburn from working the fields. Maybe Henry was right. Maybe the Germans did stick out better than the Japanese did.

By the time I spotted Audrey sitting on a worn patchwork quilt spread out under an elm, she'd already seen me. I had not seen her since the fall, and there were no remnants of the injuries she'd borne that day. She looked like any other beautiful young girl, enjoying a day at the ball field, except, I realized, that she was nearly hidden beneath the branches which had leafed out in a fierce, vibrant green.

I told Mother I was going to walk around and hopped down the rows of bleachers, sliding when I hit the wet grass. I wandered casually around behind the bleachers, searching the ground for four-leaf clovers, then drifted gradually toward the elm.

Audrey waved me over and patted the quilt agreeably. “Come sit with me,” she said, the morning air carrying the faint floral scent of her hair.

We followed the action on the field silently, until she found the nerve to say what was on her mind. “I know you know about me and David.”

I just stared at her, waiting for more. She traced her finger over the stripe in a patch of red ticking, then released the breath she'd been holding in a forceful stream. “He's gone crazy,” she said.

“What do you mean?”

She sucked the air back in and peered into the branches as if she were searching for something. “He's messing with Daddy,” she said, biting her lip.

It had been three months since David had mentioned his vague, wild plans, and I had hoped he'd forgotten all about it. “I told him to leave your daddy alone,” I hissed.

“I know. I shouldn't have never told him the things I did. Daddy got busy this spring and didn't do nothing. But now he's got time, he's got his dander up again. There's a rally after church tonight, and David says he's going.”

“I'll tell Mama. She'll stop him.”

“No!” Her blue eyes seemed to have a fire lit behind them. Her nostrils flared out as she spoke. “You can't tell nobody. It'll just make more trouble.”

“Then why are you telling me?”

“I'm just so worried,” she said, the words coming from deep in her lungs. “I got to tell somebody. But promise me you won't say nothing.”

Over her shoulder, David perched on third base waiting to run. He stood on the balls of his feet, his knees bent, his calves flexed. He leaned forward as if he would bolt any second, grinning in the direction of the batter. The air cracked wide open as the bat made contact with the ball. His smile hung in the air after he'd already disappeared off the top of the flour sack on his way to home plate.

I wanted to stop him. I wanted to run onto the field and catch him and shake him by the neck and make him promise he wouldn't do it. But I'd already tried. I only had two choices. I could help him by my silence, or betray him and possibly save his life.

David slid smoothly into home, his pants dirty, but intact. He picked himself up from the ground, dusted himself off, and sauntered triumphantly to the side of the field.

"I won't tell," I said. I meant every word, but I wasn't sure that I would be able to keep the promise.

My supper was a tense waiting game. As the wall clock ticked more loudly than I'd ever recalled, I spent my time remembering David's words that he would not be acting alone and wondering who his accomplice might be. Audrey was as frightened as I was, so I doubted she would go along with his plan. And, despite his seemingly easygoing nature, David was, in reality, somewhat of a loner when it came to anything serious. Besides, I didn't know of any of his friends who might be foolish enough to try to disrupt a Klan rally. And I was so stunned by Audrey's news, it had not occurred to me to ask where the rally would be held. If I'd wanted to intervene, I'd have not known how, other than to foil his plan altogether by telling Mother before he'd had a chance to leave camp in the first place.

My appetite had vanished and, although Mother didn't comment on it, she did give me some long looks. But she was too wrapped up in her own concerns to pry and I was tongue-tied with worry. We endured our meal in a gloomy silence.

After supper, I listened to the radio for a while, then took to the front porch with a book as a prop. Concentrating on anything other than the coming disaster was impossible. Mother appeared once to ask if I was alright and needed anything, but as I often read outdoors under the porch light on nice evenings, she had no reason to be suspicious.

The moon rose, and as it made its arc throughout the evening, its light flooded the yard from different directions. The air was filled with the usual night sounds of the owls waking up and the doves settling down. I heard Mother move about inside getting ready for bed, but out on the road and in the neighboring fields, there was no apparent activity. The last thing I recall before I fell asleep in the porch swing was the sounding of the ten o'clock hour.

The telephone ringing in our hallway woke me. With no distant family to call to catch up on our comings and goings, our telephone never rang at night, and it could only mean bad news. Anticipating disaster, I went into the house and followed the sound of Mother's voice. She stood with her back to me, the receiver pressed to her ear. She hardly moved a muscle, listening to what was being said, responding in quiet, worried murmurs. I leaned against the wall and breathed softly, trying both to hear any snippet of the conversation and to divine her thoughts.

I was able to do neither.

She replaced the receiver.

"Come with me," she said.

"What's happened?"

She pushed past me into the living room.

"Mama?" I called after her, filling the space she had just left.

Through the wall, car keys rattled, lifted from a table.

I passed through the hallway into the living room. "Mama? What's the matter?"

"David's been in a fight," she said, heading for the door.

At least he wasn't dead. "Is he okay?" I asked, shuttling closely behind her to the carport and into the passenger seat of the Buick.

She jammed the key in the ignition and stretched her arm across the seat back, easing the Buick in reverse down the drive. "He's okay." Coming to a stop in the roadway, she straightened the wheel and paused. "Sakura is in the hospital," she said, as if she expected that to answer questions rather than raise them.

"It seems she's had a nervous breakdown," she said, pressing the accelerator to the floor and kicking up a spray of gravel as we rocketed toward Camp Nine. She shook her head aggressively. "I guess it was just the last straw with that boy."

We rode to Camp Nine in silence and parked in a tiny gravel lot outside the small, clapboard infirmary. I followed her up the concrete steps and into the dim interior, where an olive-skinned nurse in a starched white uniform sat behind a metal desk. A silver goosenecked lamp perched over her appointment book and poured a circular glow onto her polished cheeks. Mother strode purposefully to the desk, pulling me along in her wake, weaving and casting like a loose leaf.

"I'm Carolina Morton," she said. "I'm here to see Sakura Matsui."

The shadow shifted across the nurse's face as she lifted her head. She pointed with a sharp pencil lead down a dark hallway. "Room 12."

"Thank you." Mother turned on her heel and faded swiftly into the gloom. I hurried along behind, our staccato footsteps punctuating the deep stillness. At the end of the corridor, an iron floor fan blew a useless stream through the hot air. Its buzz-saw insistence grew louder as we reached the middle of the hallway. Room number 12.

Mother breathed deeply and pushed open the door. Underneath an open window, Mrs. Matsui lay asleep in a hospital bed. At least I assumed she was asleep. For all I could tell, she might have been dead. David sat curled in a chair, napping, his long legs hanging over the arms, his feet crossed at the ankles. His swollen face was covered in cuts and bruises, and he'd been patched at strategic locations with white bandages that were turning pink. He looked like a broken doll.

He awoke and stiffly rearranged himself into a sitting position. I slipped into a chair, but Mother crossed the small room and stood beside the bed. "How is she?"

David raked his unkempt hair with his hand. "The doctor gave her something to make her sleep."

Mother settled herself on the side of the bed and gently tucked the sheets around Mrs. Matsui's limp form. It was the last thing she needed, I thought, as hot as it was in there.

"How'd you find out?" David asked.

She smoothed the sheet. "Colonel Jefferies called."

He winced in pain. "Thanks for coming."

She ran her fingers lightly over Mrs. Matsui's matted hair. "David . . ." There was a lecture inside her head, but she stopped herself. He was in enough trouble already. She didn't need to make it worse. "Why don't you go back to the barracks and get some rest? Did you have dinner?"

"Yes, ma'am," he said wearily, unfolding himself from the chair.

"Can I go, too?" I asked, surprising even myself.

Mother's brows narrowed.

"I don't like hospitals," I said, knowing that she'd remember that the last time I'd been in one, I'd left without a father. I felt bad pulling out a trick like that, but I wanted desperately to talk to David alone.

"David?" she said. "If you want to be by yourself, just say so. It won't hurt Chess to stay here with me."

David waved his hand at the door. "Come on, Chess. Let's go play paper dolls or something."

We left through a side door and spilled out into the warm evening air. Cricket songs pulsed from the bushes as we walked along the sidewalk.

He didn't even make me ask. His teeth gleamed in the darkness. "You should have seen it, Chess." His expression was radiant, and he bit his bloodied lip with excitement. "There was this big Klan gathering, just where Audrey said it would be. Down by Black Bayou. Everything went just as we'd planned. Except the getting-caught part."

"Who is 'we'?"

"Cottonmouth Monroe."

I was livid. "How could you get Willie mixed up in this?"

But when he told me how it had all happened, I couldn't help myself from admiring the audacity of the plan and the beauty of its execution.

Mizelle Lewis had unwittingly given them the idea. She'd been bringing her brethren regular updates concerning the apparent disintegration of Mr. Ryfle's emotional stability. His fiery sermons had grown increasingly nutty, drawing on all the imagery of the Bible. For months, he'd been treating his frightened congregation, which included all the members of his band of thugs, to his hellfire-and-brimstone rantings about the nearness of Judgment Day, the day when the devil would return to earth in the form of a snake, just as he had appeared in Eden. He was preaching that the end was near. There would be a sign, and by that sign, they would know.

Armed with this knowledge and a hand augur from Mr. Hayashida's shop, David found the rally site and the huge wooden cross that would be used, and drilled a large hole in its middle. Willie rounded up a sack of cottonmouth moccasins from Black Bayou's snake pit, charmed them quiet, and stuffed them inside. All there was left to do was to hide and wait until the climax of the ceremony, when the cross would be doused with gasoline and set afire.

So hide and wait they did, witnessing the entire proceeding from the safety of the woods. As Mr. Ryfle commenced his preaching and raging in earnest, the flames began to rise from the cross behind him, rousing the snakes, which, awakened by the heat, slithered out in massive black curls as if by cue from on high. Shocked and alarmed, Mr. Ryfle's audience routed and fled to their cars, abandoning him as he stood, rooted to his spot, and terrified of the unfolding apocalypse. Terrified of Judgment Day, that was, until he spied David escaping through the bushes. But that was the nature of David's hubris. Fooling Mr. Ryfle was not enough. David would not be content unless Mr. Ryfle knew he'd been humiliated on purpose.

"I let him catch me," David said in conclusion.

"Why?"

"To give Willie time to hide."

I couldn't believe he'd not killed David, and said so. But David might even be in worse trouble. In the struggle that followed, Mr. Ryfle was no match for the scrappy young David. David had knocked Mr. Ryfle unconscious.

"I just left him there," he said.

"Is he dead?"

"No, I just hit him hard enough to get away. But, Chess, he knows who I am. And that's why I'm leaving."

"Leaving camp? For where?"

"Detroit."

"You can't leave, David. If you stay here, he can't get to you."

"But he'll hurt Audrey. I'm going to take her away from here. Tonight."

I was stalling him, I knew. But I hoped that if some time passed, he might reconsider. "But what about your mother? Doesn't she need you?"

He released a bitter laugh. "Oh, yeah, look at her now. She's all drugged up and in the psychiatric ward of the infirmary. I heard a nurse say they didn't even have a psychiatric ward until tonight. I've done her so much good."

His smooth skin sank into his cheeks. His hair was dull and running askew. "I got Audrey into this trouble. I have to get her out of it."

"Leaving for a little while is one thing, but you can't run away—it's against the law."

He was planted on the sidewalk, his face lit with fury. "Don't you understand how crazy this life is? I don't have any control over anything. For all I know, my dad could be all the way in Japan. My mother's fallen completely apart, and I don't know if my brother's ever coming home. I can't take this anymore, Chess. I don't care what happens. I'm gone. Tonight."

He closed the gap between us, lowered his voice to an excited whisper, and told me his plan. They would go up to Detroit where Audrey had a distant cousin, and get jobs making B-24 aircraft. They would send money and messages to me for David's mother, and when the war was over, there would already be a place for her to go.

The insects glittered in the lamplight over our heads. I was suddenly caught up in his excitement. Being included in his wild plan clouded any common sense I might have normally had.

It sounded simple enough. He would go to Audrey's, but they would be too smart to try to get on a train in Rook. Besides, the next train out of Rook wouldn't be until the next morning, in broad daylight. They would walk the eleven miles into McHenry where the trains ran all night in the huge rail yard. They wouldn't ride in the compartment with everyone else because David would be spotted right away. It would be the middle of the night, pitch black, with hardly anyone working on the tracks. They would let the passenger trains go by. Down at the far end of the track, sitting all alone in the shadows, would be a freight train bound for points north. David would pick a likely car. He'd make sure that no one was around, then he'd slide back the heavy steel door and stick his head inside. It would be empty.

That was all of the story that he told me, but my imagination filled in my favorite part. He would whistle low for Audrey and she'd run, crouching between the cars to keep from being seen. He'd put his hands around her waist and boost her up into the empty railcar, then use his arms to pull himself up after her. The moonlight would glow off the door as he slid it closed. They'd find a clean spot in the hay in the back corner and lie down. He would kiss her the way I wanted his brother to kiss me.

The train would jolt as it started to move. She would rest her head against his shoulder and sleep, and when they woke up, they'd be so far gone no one would be able to find them.

I would be the only one who would know.

Chapter 16

When Tom arrived, I was sleeping fitfully on a bed of blankets and pillows the nurses had made for me on the wood floor. I smelled his aftershave in my sleep before I was aware of where I was and that he was there, speaking to Mother in a deep, rolling voice. It was her crying that woke me.

He towered next to her, clutching her arms as she sobbed into the fold of his shoulder. I knew that if I moved, they would pretend that nothing was happening, so I lay still with my eyes half open. The gold band on his finger glinted in the dark. I traced it as his hand moved along her back.

Her voice was muffled by the starched cotton and his dense muscle. She reminded him he'd promised to stay away, and asked him what he'd told Maxine.

"Nothing," he said. "I just came."

Her hair had fallen from its carefully constructed style from earlier in the night. He brushed some locks from the side of her face and kissed her neck.

I closed my eyes, knowing I wasn't supposed to see it.

"Fifteen years ago, I walked away," he said. "I should never have made that mistake. I'm not going to do it again."

Mother pulled herself from him and shook her head. "No, Tom. I meant what I said. It's over."

"What we said before, Carrie, it's wrong. We can't pretend this isn't right."

She took a deep breath, then deflated. "We both have other people to think about." She glanced at the spot where I lay, and I prayed that she didn't see my eyelashes move. "Where would we possibly fit in your life?" she said. "Of all the men in the world, Tom, you're the least free. It's not just Maxine and the girls. You're married to the army."

She pulled from his grasp. His jaw relaxed. He stood, silent, before sidling closer. "I'll leave the army. I can do something else. Anything you want. We can go away. We can go back to San Francisco if that's what you want."

She banded her arms together tightly. "No, Tom."

"Carrie, please," he said, touching her. "I'll make any sacrifices you want. Anything."

She looked to where I lay on the floor. "The sacrifices aren't ours to make."

Please, no, I thought. It was not a sacrifice. It was a gift. Please, don't let him go. Please, don't do it.

I felt that my heart wouldn't beat again until I knew. A profound pause hung, filling a gulf between them that grew wider the longer it was there. Finally, he sighed heavily, and I knew the decision was made forever.

They thought it was Mother's tugging on my arm that had awakened me, but I'd listened as the future withered before me. I let them mistake my sadness for sleepiness as we quietly filed from the room and into the thick, wet night air.

We left the Buick in the parking lot of the infirmary. Tom said that Mother was too tired to drive, and that he'd have someone deliver it to our house after the sun came up. I climbed into the backseat of a green Ford sedan emblazoned with a white star and slumped against the cushions. Mother slid in beside me, and Tom took the front seat next to his driver, an MP.

The MP started the Ford and shifted the gears, easing it onto the main road and up to the railroad crossing in the dark. The headlights jumped and scattered light in all directions as we bumped over the rails and onto Highway 1. I was tired, but I was sure I wouldn't sleep any more that night. My world had lost its bearings. I knew I didn't have any right to wish that Tom would stay and never leave, but I didn't care about what was right, even if he did have a wife named Maxine and three little children. I wanted David Matsui to stay there forever, but I knew he didn't even want to be there, and he'd probably already left for Detroit, taking Audrey with him. True love finds a way, I thought, even if some people get hurt. They just have to learn to understand.

My only consolation was Henry. The yes-yes boy. Yes, I will serve in combat duty. Yes, I will faithfully defend from all attacks, foreign and domestic. In my memory, I saw him standing straight and tall, the only one not fighting a secret. The only one fighting something else, trying to fight his way home. Against my will, I began to drift to sleep.

"Oh, Tom," Mother said, startling me awake, "can we go back?"

Tom turned around in his seat. "What's wrong?"

"I want to check on David," she said. "With everybody gone and Sakura in the hospital, I just want to make sure he's okay. Do you mind?"

I wished I'd known it was coming. If I had known that she was going to say his name, I wouldn't have let the gasp escape. She looked at me as if I'd let a curse word slip from my mouth, but she didn't comment.

As the driver turned the car in the road, my heart plunged between my ribs and landed in my lap. Maybe he was still there. Maybe he'd changed his mind entirely and decided he could wait until the war was over. Maybe we'd have a flat tire and not be able to get there. Please, Lord, I thought, I would take any miracle.

The headlights of the Ford shone directly on the charcoal tar-paper wall of the Matsuis' barracks, then they went dark, bathing us in blackness. "Y'all stay here," Mother said. "If he's managed to go to sleep, I don't want to wake him."

She quietly pulled the car door behind her. I shrank into a ball in the back seat as she climbed the wooden steps to the barracks, placed her hand on the knob, and pushed open the door, disappearing from sight.

Crickets sang. Did they ever sleep, I wondered? Normally, I would have been asleep myself, and even though I always hated to go to bed at night because I was afraid of what I might miss, I would have given my eyeteeth to have been asleep at that moment in my bed with none of it happening.

The barracks door opened, and Mother hustled loudly down the steps. She'd found the bed empty.

She leaned on Tom's window. "He's not there." She moved out of the way as Tom opened his door and unfolded himself from the Ford. "How much worse is this going to get?"

"He must be around here somewhere," Tom said, preoccupied, scanning the grounds in the darkness. "He'd better be."

I felt the blood draining out of my head. I needed to throw up, and it was happening right then. I flung open my door and tumbled to the ground, throwing up whatever it was I'd had to eat for dinner, which by then was so long ago I didn't even remember what it was.

Tom turned as Mother flew to my side. She sat in the grass beside me and held my hair until I stopped heaving. Tom knelt on one knee next to me and handed her a warm handkerchief. "Poor kid," he murmured. "This is hard on everyone."

"Chess?" Mother said, softly but sternly. "What do you know about this?"

I took the handkerchief from her hand and wiped my mouth. "Nothing," I said.

"Chess? You need to tell us the truth. Do you know where David went to tonight?"

I wanted David on that train with Audrey. I wanted them as far away from there as they could possibly get. I wanted them in a little cottage in Michigan. I wanted Tom to be my father, and I wanted Mother happy again. I wanted Henry home where we could laugh and talk about the things we loved together.

"This isn't a game," she was saying. "David's in danger. If he's left Camp Nine and he's caught by anyone other than Tom, he's going to be in real trouble. Are you hearing me?"

"Yes, ma'am."

"Are you telling me the truth that you don't know where he is?"

I wiped my mouth again and took a deep, stalling breath. "I think he was going to spend the night with one of his friends," I said, it being the only way I knew to get her off the subject, although I immediately wondered what would happen the next day when it was clear that that was not what he had done.

She exhaled relief. "Well, of course," she said to Tom, her whole body relaxing as if she'd been released by demons. "That makes perfect sense." She rose and touched her hand to her chest. "Oh, my God," she said, laughing quietly. "I feel so much better."

She reached down to help me up. "Chess, I'm sorry I doubted you." She put her arm around me. "Let's get you home and to sleep."

I slunk into the backseat of the Ford and worried only a little bit about tomorrow. By then, I might have managed to think up something else to cover for them. Then again, they'd both be so far away, no one would be able to prove that I'd been lying.

I leaned my head against Mother's shoulder as we bounced back over the railroad tracks. She looked out the window as the blackness slipped by. "I wish we'd taken his pass away from him earlier. If he hadn't been out tonight, he'd have never run across those other boys."

So that was what he'd told them. That he'd been jumped by some local boys out on the road.

"I hope to God he doesn't try anything else stupid," she said. "What would they have done to him, Tom?"

"If he were caught out without a pass?" He paused to think. "Federal prison, I guess. A work farm somewhere. Tule Lake, maybe. Whatever they want."

I felt myself getting sick all over again.

Tom's eyes reflected in the rearview mirror, trained directly on me. "If he's AWOL from a federal-detention facility, even I can't get him out of that jam."

The Ford turned into our drive and stopped in our front yard.

"Mama?" I said, my voice small and high, as if it belonged to someone else.

She squeezed me tight. "We're home, honey," she said, shuffling me off of her side. Tom exited his side and opened her door. She stepped out of the car and stretched.

I pulled myself out bit by bit and stood next to her. "I lied."

The air was so heavy, the words were suspended between us. She looked for a second like I'd slapped her, and she couldn't believe it had happened. Then she grabbed me fiercely by the shoulders. "Where?" She looked so tired and hollow I felt as though I could see through her eyes. "Where is he?"

I was so ashamed to have been caught lying in front of Tom, I felt like a foolish child. David should never have run off, and I should never have promised to keep it a secret. He was going to hate me forever if I told, and Mother was going to kill me if I didn't.

"He's gone to Audrey Ryfle's," I said, blurting it out before I had the chance to change my mind.

A look of confusion overtook her. "Whatever for?"

"They're running away. They're going to Detroit, and David's going to get a job making planes."

"Audrey Ryfle?" Her face drained of color and she turned to Tom. "Oh God, Tom."

She whirled back at me. "Chess, how could you? Why did you lie to me at Camp Nine and say he was with a friend?"

"Because . . . because, they're in love," I stammered, hoping it was the one thing that she, of all people, would understand.

"In love? Chess, they're just kids! Audrey Ryfle can't be any more than sixteen years old! And if her father were to find out . . . You have no idea what that man is capable of!" She shook her head violently. "In love," she said, spitting out the words. "You can't turn your back on everything and run away because you think you're in love. Just when you find it," she said, "it slips right through your hands. And God help you, you better have something else in your life to take its place."

Tom stood behind her, his tie loose, his sleeves rolled up around the elbows. In the lamplight, the brown hair on his muscled arms gleamed blond. There were more lines on his face than I'd ever seen.

He touched her gently. "Come on, Carrie," he said, tired and worn out. "Show me where they are."

We careened down the road that ran atop the levee. Sometimes the Ford caught a ridge of loose gravel just so, and we slid dangerously close to the edge. But our driver was capable, and soon we were upon a wide bend. In the darkness, the moonlight illuminated a clearing in the trees down below.

Mother leaned forward over the back of the front seat. "There it is," she said, pointing to a dirt road that veered off the levee and disappeared into the black night.

The Ford banked a hard left and abandoned the gravel for a dirt trail. We made a rattling bump over a cattle guard and followed the road through a tangled forest. Low branches scraped and snapped against the windows.

We made one final hairpin turn and emerged into a rough clearing. Weeds and saplings grew up and around several junked tractors and trucks. The headlights illuminated a rickety porch with three broken-down divans and a smattering of wooden chairs. A cracked chamber pot, a bicycle wheel, and a squash vine littered the steps. A soiled doll, missing both arms, dipped her head drowsily.

The MP cut the engine and we heard it immediately.

Audrey's anguished voice cut through the night. "Daddy!"

A low, dull thud sounded three times, punctuated in between each one with words.

"You!"

"Goddam!"

"Jap!"

"Daddy, stop!"

The four of us slid from the four doors of the car and bolted around the back of the Ryfles' shack, in the direction of Audrey's voice. In the back corner, a bloodied David clung to a chicken wire fence. Mr. Ryfle held a shotgun in both hands. When the butt came crashing into the side of David's head, he slumped to the ground.

Mr. Ryfle aimed his wrath at Audrey. "Your kin is off over there fighting these devils and getting kilt!" he screamed.

"We wasn't doing nothing wrong, Daddy!" Audrey said.

"Don't you back talk me, girl!" he shouted. He turned his back to her and raised the shotgun in David's direction. "I'll teach this boy to disrespect decent folk."

It was a wonder he never saw us. Tom and the MP were on him in seconds, and he fell to the ground face first, screaming and writhing like a man possessed. The MP straddled his back and subdued him with handcuffs.

Tom rose and met Mother, who was tending to David on the ground.

I heard a commotion on the porch. Six to eight little pairs of eyes peered from a window that had no screen. The door slammed, and Mrs. Ryfle stalked through the wet grass to where we stood.

"Audrey Ryfle," she said, "you git your ass back on in the house 'fore I wear you out."

Audrey eyed her viciously.

Mrs. Ryfle stood with her hands on her hips and her bottom lip thrust out. Her beady eyes shone with rage. "What the hell y'all doing here?" she said to us all. "This ain't none of y'all's business."

The MP stood, grabbed Mr. Ryfle by the handcuffs, and jerked him off the ground with one hand. "This man's under arrest."

"What fer?" she bellowed. "Don't he got a right to whup a Jap what's trying to ruin his daughter?"

The MP lifted the shotgun from the ground. "No, ma'am," he said. "He sure doesn't."

Tom rose. "Sergeant," he said, "this boy's badly hurt. Stay here with the prisoner while I run the boy to the infirmary. I'll send some others out to help you right away."

The MP raised three fingers to the bill of his cap. "Yessir."

Tom was planted square in the yard. He raised his voice so that everyone in the house could hear. "Everybody listen up!" He pointed at Mr. Ryfle. "This man is in federal custody. He is now a prisoner of the United States of America. Any attempt that any of you might make to interfere with that custody or to threaten the military police will be viewed as an act of aggression against the United States of America." He made his point directly at Mrs. Ryfle. In return, she fixed him with a vile stare.

"Come on, Carrie," Tom said. "Let's get David to the car."

The MP pushed Mr. Ryfle toward the porch. On his way past, Mr. Ryfle spit the dirt from his mouth at Mother.

"Nothin' good never did come from no Morton," he said.

Chapter 17

The old-timers said there had never been an autumn like that one. The early frost in October was followed by three straight weeks of seventy-five degrees. Mr. Hayashida predicted that, in the end, it would turn out to be a blessing. The frost ripened the rice for harvest and, with the warm weather, the winter wheat was growing like crazy.

Our tulip tree had decided that it was spring, and had broken out in crazy purple flowers. Even Grandma's stately azaleas were confused and had burst into magenta spasms. And, outside my bedroom window, my little cherry tree, not even three feet tall, had a single pink blossom clinging to the uppermost twig.

David and Mrs. Matsui had long since mended. Mother often let me go sit with David in the hospital, and I read to him from Henry's letters. I even wrote some back for him, never mentioning what had happened. A couple of weeks later, they were both released back to the barracks which Mother had cleaned to a sparkling brightness. David promised to stick close to his mother and try to give her enough stability to get her well once and for all. And he vowed to Mother that he would never leave for Detroit. At least not until his father returned, if that ever happened.

The military authority would not ordinarily have had jurisdiction over at the Ryfles' house, but since the incident involved an officer of the United States Army, they opened an investigation. How David managed to escape prosecution for leaving, I didn't know. Tom's influence was apparently still strong. But, after all was said and done, there were no charges filed against Mr. Ryfle because there was no federal law against beating someone within an inch of his life. Apparently, those matters were up to the state of Arkansas, which meant, in our corner of the world, up to the discretion of Walter Morton Sr.

But in my view, Mr. Ryfle had been lucky simply to still be alive. The MP could have shot him dead on the spot if he'd felt inclined. Neither Mother nor Tom ever learned about the Klan rally, or about David's role in disrupting it. But the snake trick played before the superstitious rabble must have essentially shut down everyone's enthusiasm for further organization, because we never heard about any further trouble.

As it turned out, Grandpa decided that Mr. Ryfle's attack on David was sufficient grounds to boot Mr. Ryfle from the farm. As soon as Mr. Ryfle was released from custody, Grandpa paid him a visit and said he would not stand for foolishness from any of his help. The Ryfle family had one month to find a new farm to work.

But Audrey was gone. She had disappeared long before her father was let go. Some people said she was hiding in Star City and styling hair there, but nobody really knew for sure. One rumor had her working in a bar out in the woods on the Saline River near Warren, and yet another was that she was being kept by a rich man in New Orleans. I wanted the last one to be true. No one in that city far to our south would have known that she came from a family of reduced circumstances. I'd seen her pass for a girl of fine breeding when she set her mind to it. I've been to New Orleans many times in the years since, and I confess having kept my eyes on the doors of cafes and shops, just in case she might walk in, decked in furs and pearls. But I never saw her that I knew of.

Tom Jefferies never again returned to Camp Nine. Within two months, Camp Nine's closing was official and had become common knowledge. Mother made excuses for Tom's absence, saying that he was busy trying to figure out what they were going to do with all the Japanese once they closed the camp, but over time, the subject faded away and died. He was not mentioned by either of us again until years later.

During her final illness, Mother wanted to clear her conscience. I let her talk, but she didn't have to tell me anything. I was a grown woman by then, and I understood well the conflict between love and motherhood. But she did tell me what I had wondered all along. Tom had been her one true love, and they had once been engaged to be married. He'd visited often then, which was how Ruby Jean knew him so well. When his family opposed their marriage on the grounds that Mother's Italian background wasn't good enough and he'd broken off the engagement, Ruby Jean, her surrogate mother, had taken it hardest of all. And Tom had married the more socially acceptable Maxine Meador, a decision he'd always regretted.

As the war wound down, the Arkansas I knew was in so many ways different than the one I'd known only two years before. One November afternoon, I lay on my bed, thinking of all that had changed since the Matsuis had come to Rook. It felt as if it had been a lifetime already and, as hard as I tried, I couldn't recall a time when they and their neighbors hadn't been a part of my life. I tried to remember what I'd thought before, what I'd hoped for, what I'd feared.

I didn't know how long I'd been asleep. In my dream, Henry and Mr. Matsui were both home, and we were sitting in church, just like the Christmas I first met them. Mrs. Matsui was there, and David ran in late, just like he did in real life. But the priest wasn't like their priest, and the church wasn't like their church. It was our church in McHenry. Everyone around me was Japanese, and they knew each other and were talking around me in a language that I didn't understand. I was confused and worried because, although it was my church, I was the stranger there, and I was afraid that someone would discover me and point me out. All around me I heard foreign words, and I didn't know what anyone was saying, but I became more anxious as the sound grew louder.

From the door of the church, a procession started, but mixed in with the altar boys were Willie Monroe and Audrey Ryfle. Willie carried the cross, and Audrey carried a large white book. Everyone in the crowd was talking among themselves as if they didn't realize that Mass was starting. As they reached the altar, Ruby Jean began yelling from the front row for Willie to get out and go home. That was no place for him, she said. "Go home," she screamed. "Go home." David got up to leave. When I asked him where he was going, he said, "Home, Chess. I'm going home."

Just then Henry, who was sitting next to me, turned. He was wearing the army uniform he wore the night he told me what a no-no boy was. He leaned in close. "Don't be afraid, Chess," he said. "I'll always be here. I'll stay at Camp Nine forever."

I awoke to the sound of the telephone ringing in the hallway. I didn't know if it was part of my dream, but just outside my window, in the silent moment between asleep and awake, I heard a sigh. A sweet, soft, sad, whispering sigh that floated to the ground like a feather.

I sat up straight and slid my legs over the side of the bed and listened, but all I could hear was Mother's voice. I got up so slowly I felt as though I was walking underwater.

She was pressed against the wall with the telephone to her ear and her hand to her heart. I slipped past her out the back door of the porch, and across the yard to the fence. It seemed to be a thousand steps to where I was going and my body was fighting its way through a thick fog.

I fell to my knees and gently lifted the single pink blossom from the splintered green grass where it had fallen.

Mother stood in the yard and wiped the back of her hand across her eyes. I was only hearing snippets of what she was saying. Somewhere in France, Henry Matsui had vanished, missing in action.

I cradled the blossom in my hands, but the tears wouldn't come.

Mr. Hayashida dropped the shovel and knelt beside me in the dirt. The cold front that had blown through had suddenly made it winter all over again, but we were sheltered against the wind by a concrete monument. The number "442" loomed above our heads. I patted my gloved hands into the dirt around the base of the little cherry tree. "Do you think it'll grow here?"

Mr. Hayashida touched a graceful branch. "Oh, yes," he said. "This is where it was meant to be. It will be here when you and I are long gone. It has to. It has to look over these boys."

Camp Nine's imminent closing was now a mixed blessing to David. With Henry missing, David had nowhere to pin his hopes. Henry was neither there at Camp Nine, nor on an Italian mountainside. There would be no more letters. Only dreams that a miracle would occur, and he would someday reappear. David imagined him in Europe somewhere, behind barbed wire just as they were. But Henry's words, which I kept to myself, haunted me. "Camp Nine forever."

Mr. Hayashida stood and held out his hand to me. My knees ached as I rose, but eventually they stopped hurting as we walked away from the cemetery through the winter grass of the brown field toward Camp Nine.

Mrs. Matsui sat staring ahead in her seat. Although I couldn't see her small hands, she held her back straight such that they must have been folded in her lap.

A crying, laughing, shouting crowd pressed around me. A burst of steam signaled that it was finally all over. The train groaned heavily, and the wheels started as if they'd been awakened from a dream that had lasted too long.

David leaned out the window, his cap pulled rakishly over that same shock of glossy black hair that fell forward over his eye.

He called out to me. "Goodbye, Chess!"

I waved to him and crossed my arms over my chest, as a warm, early-morning summer breeze blew across my face. They started slowly, then picked up speed toward McHenry, growing smaller. David took off his cap and waved it in the smoky air. He thrust his head farther out the window. "Come see us in Chicago!"

I stood in the soft dirt by the tracks.

"Promise?" he called out.

I promised. I didn't know then that it would be so many years before I saw David again.

Camp Nine would be gone as fast as it had come. The barracks and the kitchens, the classrooms and the living rooms, the storage sheds and the garden sheds, all broken down and carted off and sold away, reduced to nothing more than pennies on the dollar. The proud city of the Americans who were also Japanese vanished into the rich, black Delta summer as if none of it had ever been.

All that remained was the cemetery. It stood alone in the cotton field with the names of the men of the 442nd carved into the cold concrete slab. The ghosts were stilled and the dreams were long gone.

Even now, the cherry blossoms burst and fall with no one to hear them.

The envelope is yellowed and addressed in the careful hand of a person for whom the English alphabet was learned later in life. A creased black and white photograph of a man, a woman, and a teenaged boy standing in front of a shabby block of apartment buildings sticks to the faint remnants of glue. There is not one smile among them, but they pose gamely for the unknown photographer, perhaps a new neighbor, perhaps a passing stranger. The letter itself is written by someone else, someone impatient, for whom this task needs to be completed so that he can move on to something else.

April 6, 1946

Dear Carrie,

I have asked David to write you this letter for me to tell you that we are here in Chicago. The resettlement people have put us in a temporary place until we can get enough money to live some place better. But at least it is a real building with bricks and windows that do not let the insects inside.

Hiroshi is home now. They closed Tule Lake. He knows of your petitions for his release and he thanks you for trying.

I'm afraid times are very hard. We have to start over with nothing and he would not want to know that I have told you this, but there is no work for Hiroshi because of Tule Lake. I think there is something wrong now. He will not leave his bed. I thank God for David, but I am ashamed that we cannot send him to college. He has a job working, thank goodness, and he takes care of the family now.

I will write to you again when we have a permanent home.

Your friend,
Sakura Matsui

It was the last we heard.

1965

In person, David Matsui looks younger than his thirty-eight years. A strand of silver streaks his jet black hair, grown long in the new mod fashion. He removes the fitted blazer of his neat Edwardian suit and folds it across his arm. His crisp, white shirt has wilted a bit above the slim trousers. A narrow, dark tie is knotted around his neck loosely and carelessly. He looks every bit the part of the artist who has grown very wealthy.

He closes the door of the Jaguar convertible, dust collecting on the tops of his leather shoes. "So, that little tree really did grow."

I think of the many differences between us at this moment. The one I can't get past is that I know so much about him, and he so little about me. As I take in his image, all the bits and pieces I've collected about him from magazines and newspapers run together like threads building a tapestry that matches the man standing in front of me. But it is my own face I see reflected in his dark glasses. "I like your car," I say, the only topic that seems innocuous enough to offer as an opening.

"I don't keep a car in the US anymore," he says after a moment. It may be only my imagination that he emphasizes the last word. "I borrowed it from a friend in Memphis."

The barrier of his impenetrable glasses is unsettling.

"It's very nice," I say.

He looks at the sleek machine as if he's never seen it before, but he doesn't answer. He pulls at his already slack tie, and walks past me along the gravel path that leads into the cemetery. As the sun beats down on his shirt, I'm annoyed that he's dressed so formally, as if he's in costume for a performance.

I wait a moment, then follow. "David?"

He slows as he makes his way past a row of headstones. It's no effort to catch up to him.

He reaches the concrete monument to Henry's battalion, handmade by Edo Hayashida so long ago, then turns suddenly. "I heard about your mom," he says.

Mother. I can't imagine who would have told him of her death. "I didn't know how to reach anyone," I say, not knowing myself what that meant. Who would I have told who wasn't already aware, as small as our community is? "How did you hear?"

"Your local telegraph office rejected my telegram to her."

How things had changed. Telegrams were no longer handled by Mr. Gilwell, who had passed ten years or more ago. They were now routed through McHenry, and there was talk of closing that office as well.

"So I located Tom Jefferies. He's a general now. He saw it in the Little Rock paper and said you were still around here, in Dante."

My mind goes to a faraway memory. Tom Jefferies would be so much older now, his hair gray like my mother's was when she died. I'm glad I haven't seen him. I want to remember him the way he was then, young and straight, his arms strong and protective. But a general. Mother was right. He was married to the army.

David takes a step sideways, into the shadow of the tank-shaped monument.

"And your mother?" I say, the intention hanging in the air.

His jaw moves slightly. "She's gone," he says. "My mother and father, they're both gone."

We stare at each other.

"I'm so sorry," I say.

He turns his back on me and inspects the monument. He looks up at the names inscribed in the concrete, his arms hanging stiffly by his side. "They never got over it," he says.

I feel the indictment of his anger directed at me. I wonder if David ever knew of my family's unwitting role in bringing them here, if he had ever sensed that the land that had imprisoned his family had once been, and was, once again, in my name. I had never wondered that before.

Perhaps it's defensiveness that emboldens me, but whatever it is, I'm angry at his posturing. "David," I say sharply.

He looks at me with surprise.

"For heaven's sake, take off your glasses. I can't see you."

He hesitates, then reaches up slowly and removes them.

He's seventeen again.

His body relaxes. He hangs the dark glasses on his collar, and his hands go in his pockets.

"Did you borrow the clothes, too?" I ask, provoking that familiar grin I haven't seen in so many years.

He lowers his head and his hair falls over his eye. "No. But sometimes it feels like it."

"It's good to see you again," I say.

"You, too." He walks away from me, running his fingertips over the headstones. I wander after him. "What about you, Chess?" he says. "What did the years bring you?"

It strikes me as an odd way to phrase the question. I can't tell if he wants a complete answer or if he's only being polite. "I left Rook for college up east," I say, "heard a familiar accent one day at a Yale party and met my husband, who's from outside Dante. We have two girls. We both farm."

"So, you stayed after all," he says.

"There was no one else to take over the place." It's the truth, but as I say it, I realize I'd never considered any other choice. I should have wanted to leave. I should have wanted to sell the land and live a sophisticated, exciting life in a distant city, but the Delta is in my blood. No other place could ever be home. I had taken meeting my husband in a happenstance way in such a foreign place as the Northeast as a sign.

"I waited for letters from you," I say.

Above our heads, a stone eagle spreads its wings. David looks upward. "I tried to write a couple of times. But there wasn't anything to say."

"I wanted to know," I say. "We wanted to know what happened to you." I pause. "And to Audrey."

He gazes across the vacant field. "I don't know what happened to Audrey."

"Didn't you ever try to find her?"

Behind us a mockingbird trills. "We all wanted to forget, Chess. There was so much shame involved. All we could do was try to move on."

He isn't going to tell me anything. I know that I need to just take pleasure in the fact that he is here. Now. "Well," I say, forcing my cheerfulness, "you've done very well for yourself. We gave you your music. At least that's something."

He nods. "That's true, you did. But it was a tough road getting there."

I've hit on a subject he's receptive to, and I sense an opening. I settle onto a stone bench. "David, if you're willing, I'd love to hear about it."

He folds his lanky frame next to me and grins. "When we got to Chicago, there were lots of guys playing the blues. You know, black guys that had come from all over the South. Mississippi, mostly. I started hanging around clubs, sitting in on the sides, just listening." He laughs at the memory. "I guess I looked pretty funny in there. There were *no* Asians. Barely any white faces at all, except for the club owners and a few executives from the record companies. But a couple of the old guys were from the Arkansas side, as they called it. When they found out I learned the blues from Cottonmouth Monroe, they treated me like one of their own."

"They knew Willie?"

He becomes animated. "Knew him—Chess, they revered him. He was famous. There's this music historian, he's my neighbor in London, but in the forties and fifties, he went all around the South trying to record the old masters. He tried to get to Willie, but he told me that Willie's niece wouldn't let him on the property. Said she didn't want any trouble."

I laugh hard. "Ruby Jean?"

"Yeah, Ruby Jean ran him off. Said she threatened to call Mr. Morton on him."

I have to catch my breath. "Oh, my God," I say, clutching my hand to my throat. "I had no idea! But can't you just see it?" Our laughter dies down. "Mother never told me about that."

David gives me a swift, sideways glance. "Your mother wouldn't have known. Ruby would have been too afraid to tell your family that anyone was coming around, wanting to record 'race music.' White and black never crossed. That's the way it was. You tried to tell me that once, in your own way. I didn't believe you."

Ruby Jean's fierce protection of Willie and his music comes back to me in a flurry of long-forgotten scenes. I had thought she was trying to protect me. But it was Willie she was shielding. How could I have not known these things? Was there really so much going on around me that I didn't understand?

"We weren't oblivious to everything," I say, a dash of defensiveness flavoring the edge of my voice.

David faces me squarely. "Oh, yeah? Besides me, name me one bluesman."

He grins at my loss for words.

"See? Lived your whole life in the Arkansas Delta, and you can't name me one bluesman. And you know why? Because you're a cultured, white woman. But I'm not white, Chess. I always thought I was, growing up. But I didn't really know what white was until the United States government carved us out of the white race, set us on a plate, and served us up into a dark corner of Arkansas. That's when I learned what white really is. It's separate. It's sheltered. It's a race apart."

The truth of his words lessens their sting, but my face burns knowing that he'd most likely said these things about us to the strangers he's met. I recall defending my southern ways to girls in college who'd surprised me with their assaults on my culture, a part of me I'd never thought to question.

David takes my hand. "Please don't take any of this as an attack on you. I'm just saying that you didn't appreciate what treasures you had here, right under your nose." He shakes his head. "I didn't understand how priceless somebody like Willie was, either. Not while it was happening."

I realize sadly that I haven't thought of Willie in years. He'd died over a decade ago. A flu epidemic that caused most of us a mild inconvenience was fatal to an old man living in a drafty shack.

"Willie's gone," I say.

"I figured," he says. He tugs on his tie. The knot comes loose and the two tails fall forward over his knees. "Willie was the real deal."

"You know what Ruby Jean used to say about him?" I ask. "She said that God doesn't take away but what He gives back double."

"Because he was blind?"

"Yeah. Do you think that's true? That since he was born blind, he had a deeper connection to his music?"

He blinks at me in surprise. "He wasn't born blind."

"Yes, he was."

His eyes narrow. "No, he wasn't."

"Yes. His mother had yellow fever. He was blind his whole life."

He looks at me intently. "That's what you heard?"

"It's the truth."

He stands and walks a few steps, his hands on his hips. Then he turns. "Here's the truth, Chess. Here's what nobody apparently told the poor, little rich girl. Willie Monroe could see perfectly fine until the day your levee foreman beat him half to death in a drunken rage."

I stand as well. "That's not true!"

"Oh, yes it is. That's the kind of thing that goes on around here that nobody wants to talk about." He stretches out his arms, indicating the entirety of the Camp Nine site. "There are all kinds of things that go on around here that nobody wants to talk about. It wasn't yellow fever, it was Charlie Ryfle."

Charlie Ryfle. "Mr. Cholly," I say absently. "The meanest foreman on the Arkansas side."

"That's right. Mr. Cholly. Willie got him in trouble with the animal agency up in Memphis about his mules. They hit Charlie with a fine, and he beat Willie so savagely there was blood coming from his eyes and his ears."

Blood.

"What happened to Charlie Ryfle?"

"Willie said that any law on the levee was Mr. Morton's law."

The bad blood.

"Your grandpa sent a squad out to get Charlie. They shot him to death and dumped him on that Indian mound out there."

I sink to the concrete bench. I am outraged that no one had ever told me the truth, but I realize there is no one left to be angry with. They are all gone. Ruby Jean, Willie, Grandpa, and even Mother, although I wonder if she ever knew the truth herself.

"Why didn't Ruby Jean want me to know?" I ask, as much to myself as to David.

"Are you serious? Can you really not comprehend all this?" I'm stunned by what seems to be real fury on his part. "Chess, this is the Delta. This is a crazy, dangerous place. The things that happen here shouldn't happen to people. Anywhere. And your family—the Mortons—they were at the center of it. You were just a sheltered little girl. How could you have handled that kind of responsibility?"

I'm no longer that little girl, but I suddenly feel foolish to even have been who I was. He is right. How could I have comprehended the pain that was, and still is, a daily part of life here?

He rubs the top of his head, then shakes it. "I'm sorry, Chess. I don't know. I guess Ruby Jean raised your mother. She loved you all. Maybe she didn't want to believe you could be one of those people."

He sits next to me again. "That was what was so special about your mother, Chess," he says, his voice barely a whisper. "She wasn't like everybody else. She cared. She wasn't afraid to come out here and try to make a difference."

An image of the lies that swirled around my young life forms before me like a spider web. I want to go back. I want to see things again with a new view. I want the chance to act out my part with a new understanding of the stories of the other players. I now understand Mother's fear of Mr. Ryfle. I now understand Grandpa's reluctance to let him go, the boy he orphaned. I now understand Willie's blues.

I know that Camp Nine was something that should never have been. It destroyed lives and separated families; it interrupted joys and brought, in their stead, wretched sorrows. But the experience was mine, too. On a deeper level than I had ever understood, Camp Nine had defined my life. The misery of thousands had shone a light on who I was, on who we all were, here in the Delta. Would I have ever known these things without their sacrifice?

There is still an unanswered question. "Why did you come here today?"

"You haven't asked about Henry," he says.

Henry. My lost hero. Could it be possible that he's alive?

My pulse quickens. "Where is he?"

He stands again, pausing. "He died in France at Biffontaine."

Lightheaded, I grip the edges of the bench. "How do you know?"

He thrusts his hands in his pockets and paces. "For years, I looked for him. I went all over Europe, trying to find lists of German prisoner-of-war camps. But I could never find his name anywhere. Then one day about a month ago, I'm playing a gig in Paris, and this guy comes up to me. A fan. He was in the 442nd with Henry. He was one of the guys Henry saved that day. He wanted to thank me."

"But he was missing in action. How do you know he died?"

"This guy saw him. He knows he was dead. But the guy was wounded himself, and they evacuated him out. He said no one ever asked him. He thought I knew."

There is nothing to do but feel my insides sink.

"I cancelled all my gigs in Paris. I got a car and drove out to Biffontaine. The battlefield was easy to find. That's the only reason anybody ever goes there. I found the place where the guy said Henry died, a place called Suicide Hill. I sat down with my guitar and just sang all through the night until the next morning."

He closes his eyes and rocks gently, his face swaying to a rhythm inside his head. His voice, when he sings, is like gravel churning inside a bucket.

Ain't but the one thing I done wrong.
Ain't but the one thing I done wrong.
Aint' but the one thing I done wrong,
Stayed in Arkansas jes' a day too long.
Day too long, lawdy, jes' a day too long.

He falters to a stop.

A breeze rustles the leaves of the trees that ring the cemetery. The quiet is broken only by the cicadas.

His eyes open, but the young boy of moments ago has disappeared. "And then I knew I had to come here. I've run as long as I can. I'm done." He sizes up the grounds, then strides across the grass toward the cherry tree.

"Where are you going?" I call out to him, but he doesn't answer. I get up and follow.

When he reaches the tree, he stops, his feet planted in a sea of pink blossoms, and peers up into the branches. "I guess this is as good a place as any," he says.

From underneath the blazer, he pulls out Henry's senninbari and tenderly unfolds it. Mother's tiger is barely visible now, faded by the years. But the stains of Henry's blood, now black, will never fade. They run in uneven streaks across the panels. David selects two lesser branches, and threads their tips through the senninbari.

"The guy in Paris brought it with him. Said, all these years, he didn't know how to find us."

From his pocket, he pulls out a blue ribbon and pins it to the delicate, discolored fabric. He slips his dark glasses over his eyes and begins the walk to his car.

"What is it?" I ask.

He stops in the gravel. "It's what Henry deserved," he says over his shoulder.

I look at the ribbon closely. Tiny white stars are pasted onto the ribbon and a cardboard bronze eagle clutching the word "valor" dangles in the breeze, a crude imitation of the Medal of Honor.

He faces the cemetery. "Why is it that men like Henry could look past what was done to us and go out there and fight and die, but this nation couldn't get past the way we looked?"

He opens the car door, and sunlight flashes from the window. "Listen, Chess," he says, "I'll always remember you and your mother. I'll never forget the kindness you showed us. And I guess now is the time to say the thank you I never said. But now you know why I live in London."

As I stand in the shade of the cherry tree, he slides into the car and closes the door behind him. The engine purrs aggressively as he makes a neat turn in the road and drives slowly away from me, leaving me alone with the senninbari and the handmade medal. I study them both, observing the care with which they were made. I think of the love that went into David's creation of the amateurish token, the musical genius, the hurt little boy, the confused man, still fighting for justice, just as his fallen brother had. Each of them had carried a bit of my Delta to the world, and they were now both lost to me forever.

As a feverish gust of wind comes in off the cotton, pale blossoms swirl around me like snow. The senninbari hangs in the tree, but the cardboard and its ribbon lift from the branch and pause. Mixed with the petals, they float on the current, dip in the air, then fall down into the white dust of Camp Nine.

VIVIENNE SCHIFFER grew up in the Arkansas Delta town of Rohwer, site of the Rohwer Relocation Center, on which *Camp Nine* is based. She is an attorney and has practiced law for twenty-eight years in Houston, where she lives with her husband Paul and their family. Schiffer is currently at work on her second novel.